PRAISE FOR HUG

T0266214

"Hugo Charteris was among the m[
postwar generation and *The Tide Is Right* (which was never p~~~~~
his lifetime) is one of his best books. He wrote, in my opinion, more
truthfully about the upper classes than any of his contemporaries. This
study of family jealousy and dispossession in an old Scottish landowning
family is as exciting as a thriller but its qualities are more than purely
narrative. The people and the place are seen with an unmatched intensity
and brought to life by a distinctive prose style of rare beauty and extraordinary expressive power." —Francis Wyndham

"*The Tide Is Right* is one of Charteris's more elusive books, with a
wonderfully perceptive view of upper-class Scottish life. He is, I think,
undoubtedly one of the most original, quirky, and shrewd explorers of
the behaviour of the landed gentry among postwar English novelists,
and at a time when prose was plain, his was idiosyncratically stylish,
capable of suggesting comedy, tragedy, and romance with fastidious
economy." —Alan Ross, *London Magazine*

"Mr. Hugo Charteris is a curious novelist, an odd man out among his
generally predictable contemporaries. He is both original and banal,
straightforward and complicated, topical and old-fashioned, derivative
and original; a Greene obsessed with irrelevancies, a Firbank who reads
the newspapers, an elusive, allusive, elliptical writer with the courage to
tackle glaringly obvious problems head-on, and the ingenuity to stand
them on their heads." —Francis Hope, the *Observer*

"Hugo Charteris's novels have a flavour of melancholy which resolves
itself into ironical comedy . . . a prevailing sense of a class, a society,
decomposing . . . well written and well observed, in places very funny,
full of shrewd comment on our times." —Malcolm Muggeridge, the
Observer

OTHER NOVELS BY HUGO CHARTERIS

A Share of the World (1953)

Marching with April (1956)

Picnic at Porokorro (1958)

The Lifeline (1961)

Pictures on the Wall (1963)

The River-Watcher (1965)

The Coat (1966)

The Indian Summer of Gabriel Murray (1968)

Hugo Charteris

THE TIDE IS RIGHT

Introduction by Nicholas Mosley

Dalkey Archive Press

Library of Congress Cataloging in Publication Data
Charteris, Hugo.
    The tide is right / Hugo Charteris; introduction by Nicholas Mosley.
    I. Title.
PR6053.H373T53   1991   823'.914—dc20   90-14062
ISBN: 0-916583-71-6 (cloth)
ISBN: 0-916583-78-3 (paper)

First paperback edition, 1992

The author wishes to acknowledge with gratitude permission to quote some lines from
a poem by Kathleen Raine which appeared in *The Year One,* published by Hamish
Hamilton.

Partially funded by grants from The National Endowment for the Arts and
The Illinois Arts Council.

Dalkey Archive Press
1817 North 79th Avenue
Elmwood Park, IL 60635 USA

"Then goeth he, and taketh to him seven other spirits more wicked than himself; and they enter in and dwell there: and the last state of that man becometh worse than the first."

—Luke 11:26

" 'The almost fossilized state of our recollection is attested to by our murderers and those who read every detail of crime with a passionate and hot interest,' the doctor continued. 'It is only by such extreme measures that the average man can remember something long ago; truly, not that he remembers, but that crime itself is the door to an accumulation, a way to lay hands on the shudder of a past that is still vibrating.' "

". . . In the king's bed is always found, just before it becomes a museum piece, the droppings of the black sheep."

—Djuna Barnes, *Nightwood*

Introduction

HUGO CHARTERIS was a British writer who was born in 1922 and died in 1970. He wrote eight novels, two children's books, and several plays for television. He was making his name as a writer at the same time as the "angry young men" were becoming fashionable in the 1950s. The angry young men railed against what they saw as the class-ridden values of an out-of-date Britain; they became fashionable because they were partisan and simplistic. Hugo Charteris was not an angry young man, in that in his novels he tried to describe the complexity of changing attitudes of a class-conscious Britain from the inside. He himself came from an aristocratic background and he wrote not only of the absurdities and irrelevances typical of the British aristocracy but also of the resilience, the earthiness and even ruthlessness that would enable it in a modified form to survive. Thus he could not be aligned with the current anti-establishment fashion, but neither could he be easily approved of by the British upper classes who seemed to feel themselves threatened by an exposure of their toughness and cunning as well as of their absurdities, whereas they could look down on the angry young men as clowns.

The Tide Is Right was Hugo Charteris's third novel; it was due to be published in England in 1957. It was at page-proof stage when word got round that the subject matter was recognisably to do with the antics or potential antics of a notable British aristocratic family: one or two members of the publishing house were members of the so-called old boy net. Hugo Charteris was travelling in the wilds of West Africa at the time; when he got home he found that the publication of his book had been stopped. A proof copy of the book had been sent to a member of the aristocratic family; the two persons in real life from whom the chief protagonists of the story were said to have been drawn had themselves made no objections to publication; Hugo Charteris was friendly with both, and had joked with at least one of them about the contents of the story. But other members of the family who could not be said to come into the story at all were claiming that the family had been insulted; so-and-so had had a quiet word with so-and-so at the very highest level of the publishing and aristocratic worlds; and the book was effectively dead. Hugo Charteris said that he was ready to change anything that in law could be said to be libellous; he even experimented with changing the story's environment from Scotland to Wales. But after the quiet words in high places, and his own joking half-admissions, no English publisher would risk taking on his novel. What Hugo had described about the not-so-latent ruthlessness of the British upper class was indeed being demonstrated.

It seemed to be then and seems to me now that *The Tide Is Right* is a very good novel and that it was a tragedy that it did not have the chance to be recognised as such when it was written. In all Hugo Charteris's novels there is a boldness of style and wit and characterisation that is both funny and touching; but *The Tide Is Right* has a conciseness of structure and a precise story line that were not always typical of his novels, but which here raise the story to that level at which characters seem to be involved with fate. Halfway through the book one of the two chief protagonists, Alan, says of the other: "Look. Two hundred years ago do you know what Duncan would have 'done tomorrow'? He would have rubbed me out. Like *that*." And Alan makes "a slow precise pinching gesture" with his finger and thumb. Alan, for all his self-protection behind a comic mask, knows that his family have not changed much in two hundred years; also that one of the characteristics of his family is not to worry too much about the chances of an individual member being rubbed out.

Even before *The Tide Is Right* Hugo Charteris had the reputation of someone who wrote potentially libellous novels about real people; he continued to be haunted by this reputation for the rest of his life. Many of those affected were brave enough to ignore or to surmount imagined hurts and slights; others—usually those most dependent on the facades of prestige and power—were not: at least one other novel was banned through threat of legal action. Hugo Charteris himself through all this maintained an attitude that could be called either innocently optimistic or blind: he used to say that he could not understand why the people supposed to being represented by his characters should mind; did they not know how serious fiction writers had always worked? and why should it be hurtful to people to be able to look at some of their own odd corners in the general comedy of human life? In the 1960s Hugo Charteris met the psychologist C. J. Jung, of whom he had long been an admirer. Might it not reasonably be argued that there was no evil in people being able to look at their shadow side?

I myself had become a close friend of Hugo Charteris by the time of *The Tide Is Right*. I had first come across him at school where he had seemed a solitary, somewhat puritanical figure in our world of slyness and horseplay; what I had learned about him was that his mother had died when he was young and he had been brought up to some extent as an orphan in the huge houses of grandparents and aunts. Then during the 1939-45 war he was an officer in the Scots Guards and he won the Military Cross in Italy; after the war he married and worked for a time as a journalist; it was then that I began to know him well. He went with his wife and young children to a small house on the east coast of Scotland and tried to earn his living as a writer of novels and scripts and short stories. Being the son of a younger son he had no inherited money of his own; the friends who lived on large estates around him were generous; but then he was apt to put them into his novels. It seemed that in spite of all his insights and honesty there was something he never quite recognised about his own attitude to the society into which he had been born; he both loved and hated this more than he knew. He remained part of a world that pays lip service to writers but is not at ease with them; that perhaps has to protect itself in its own way. What he loved about this world was its earthiness—the ritualistic contacts between masters, workers and animals on large country estates. What in his books he mocked—but perhaps did not see the steeliness in his mockery— was the inability of some people in this world, so tough in their dealings with the environment, to be brave about themselves. He went on imagining that he and those about whom he wrote could settle for the best in each other. But he himself had written of the pain and complexity of people trying, or indeed of refusing to try, to look into themselves.

I last saw Hugo in the summer of 1970 when I was in bed after a bad car accident and he came to visit me; it was known to his friends then that he was probably dying of cancer. Some time before this, the chief protagonists of one of his novels had been seen to be based on my wife and myself; he had wondered if we would mind; we had not minded; what strange tricks the characters got up to! but then, what a matter of circus tricks was life! Now, on my sick bed, Hugo came to cheer me up. He was the most wonderful raconteur; he told me of the bizarre goings-on of his acquaintances and relations; of the outrage caused by his latest television play. There was also the wild and unpredictable behaviour of some of the organs of his body, was there not; almost as unhinged as that of some of the members of the old boy net. His style was quiet and brave and humourous and ironic; he was always, and especially at the end of his life, what could be called a beautiful man. Most of the protagonists of his books would have been brave about dying; what they had not been so good about was the business and cost of looking at life.

NICHOLAS MOSLEY

The Tide Is Right

PART ONE

1

IT WAS the year of the extraordinary winter.

An hour before dawn a big American car turned off the main road at the point where the Pole had inked up a cardboard notice "To the hatchery." The headlights dawdled on the leggy lettering, and the bodywork hung over as the inside wheels went deep in slush. Then, with a brief rushing asperity from the engine and a thrashing of chains the huge resilient shape went creaking and rocking down the track.

After two hundred yards of gentle downward slope the car passed a long squat building with a sixty-foot chimney stack, which looked like the Last Factory. No road or path seemed to lead off towards it but a single bulb burnt low down and sometimes proved occupation and activity, even at this hour, when a shadow crossed it and was thrown a mile.

The car reached a big clearing and began to turn, shunting back and forth.

The thaw was in its second day. Brown slush flew up round the racing wheels; but with it came a spray of clinker and small coal and this probably explained the confidence of the driver, turning in such a place.

When still, the car vanished as head and rear lights went out.

Then a match sprouted at the steering-wheel . . . dwindled and spurted at the end of a cigar, revealing by fits and starts, a round rather puffy face which might have been a middle-aged woman's, cupped as it was in a veritable ruff of polar-necked sweater and thatched with hair long enough to curl in scimitars behind the ears, and at the nape develop the baroque tufts and convolutions of a duck's arse.

When the glowing tip was still it took its place in a confused galaxy of pinprick lights: the last stars above Port Alford, the radar masts, a few cottages on the lower hills, the first and the night-long lights in the town—and also, without perceptible division, the double of all these reflected in the vast intervening stretch of saturated mud. The eye, therefore, could not rest with certainty on any part of the darkness and name its nature.

Brisk puffs of wind made a tree rustle and sometimes roar, but in the lulls the wind seemed not to have stopped at all until the car sensed the eternal rustle to be another kind—the fluent liquidity of a great mass of water, not very far away.

The cigar tip stirred from time to time.

In the east now there seemed to lie the reflection of a neon-lighted city; and soon, the clouds overhead were slowly defined like the fouled, waste smoke of an expended explosion—night—now receding—dissipating and sapping identity and perspective with every minute that passed, from what was immense, magic and immeasurable; and letting the day suggest labels for close dank and relevant objects.

The man inside the car peered upward like a person from a shelter assessing the amount of rain still to come. Then he got out.

He was scarcely five-foot-three.

He fumbled with a torch. The beam wandered over khaki scarves, cartridges, gunstock, suddenly probed into the interior and revealed shabbiness and mess inside the huge deluxe hull.

He swore in a way that is more usual in military company—the monosyllables being arranged with artistic care and carefully pronounced.

Because his balaclava was in the boot.

As he worried round the car he made it look like the loot of a pygmy.

Ready at last he was swathed fat as a diver, only his nose, eyes and outer finger-joints bare. A kilt peeped between oilskin and waders with oddly festive colour and abundance.

He set off fast—only using his torch once or twice to find a gap in wire and cross a plank bridge.

On the edge of the mud he stopped.

To the east the skylined dawn was exactly as in B.C. This, in some way, seemed to account for the presence, at such an hour, of a man whose lit face was a pouched mask of sybaritic laziness. For a gleam in his dull, inexpressive eye, as he raised his face to the breeze, suggested a second-nature familiarity with eternal sea, dawn, desolation and, paradoxically, discomfort.

And this gleam endowed him, for an instant, with an identity superior to the diffident pomposity which had lately possessed his features during the search for his balaclava. The gleam belonged to him, perhaps, only here.

He moved his head slowly, facing this way and that.

A single, distant note, like a tenor's, intoned the word "encre." It was not repeated.

After ten minutes' stillness, the little lonely figure set out across the mud.

Each step made a noise of harsh suction and his course was heavily marked by the dotted line of his footmarks.

A few widgeon were on the move now. Their wings and plaintive double-noted whistle seemed to give warning of a stranger's presence; but in fact they were behaving as usual.

The Cass River runs down a creek in the centre of the estuary. On a spring tide, if there's a spate, the river surface is flush with the mud waste.

So he came to where the mud seemed suddenly to have become mobile—not just ahead—but as far as the eye could see, to right and left, and in front. It swept by with an immense whisper and occasional swallowing noises, the surface marked with great blisters of smoothness which retained their shape as they went down—and with scribbles revolving in a movement of their own.

Turning inland and upstream he faced the south-eastern sky. A small tree, pared down by force to its trunk and thickest branches, had been swept just so far and then stuck. There, like a vast Chinese character turned on its side. it put a jet pattern on the pale screen of the dawn. One dislocated limb in particular stood out with a crude, functional apartness from the main organic symmetry.

"Encre encre," then another note higher and different as though a donkey were about to bray. Then silence.

The small figure moved out into the water and at once his boots threw up bow-waves. He trod carefully, feeling forward, until the water was over his knees. He stopped. The bow-waves danced round his thighs and he had to cradle his gun, high, in the crook of his arm.

A few enthusiasts know that this is the place at Port Alford to get the geese. When movement starts in the town and along the sea-wall the birds, which roost in the hags right against the town's edge, all rise and swing back, out to sea.

The hieroglyph tree was dead upstream from the small human figure, and the dislocated branch was attached below the water, unless it were part of a different tree, or something by itself.

He cannot have had much else to look at for the next half-hour except this strangely shaped dead limb which stuck out. He may perhaps have been asleep—with his eyes open. It is easy to get into that sort of state there.

The moving water against the dawn takes on the leaden sheen of a dead eye. The eddy patterns emerge into focus and pass with hypnotic effect. The bow-wave at your boots rushes loudly, soporifically, and there is something almost wooing in the consistent massive thrust which strokes your legs.

The shore-shooters wait for a certain moment when night and dawn are finished; when sickly, clammy day is declared, by lights in rows in the town—when intimations of false teeth, shaving, voiding the body and the mouth and the rhythmic crash of milk-bottle cages in the street mark a prelude for most people's monotony. Faintly the sounds of this time reach the middle of the estuary. They coincide with enough light to see pairs, trios, parties of fast high duck crossing and recrossing the sky on no particular line.

It was at this moment on this particular day of the year that in front of the little figure, suddenly, the grey vacancy of moving water became marked with a dark shape.

It came nearer. Something floating. A branch.

He moved slightly to let it have a wider berth. It went by and as it passed revealed its size and speed.

At once he began to wade fast towards the bank and he was doing this when a noise like two shots, fired almost simultaneously, stopped him.

Upstream the tall, functional, dislocated limb of the stranded tree had disappeared.

It had not been thick—nowhere near as thick as the thing which had just gone by. But mere slow sustained pressure of water could not conceivably have snapped it in that sudden, loud way.

The little man began to run—or rather plunge, hobbled knee-high by water—for the muddy edge.

The shallows came so suddenly he tripped. Regaining his balance he walked backwards a few more steps, looking back at the water.

At this moment the geese rose.

For a few seconds they seemed to challenge each other to do so, some refusing some encouraging—then all at once innumerable voices said one thing: go; whereupon the roar of wings was added to the clamour.

Then there was sudden silence and lightness as striking as the moment when the runway and hangars appear below, impersonal and remote.

The occasional honk now sounded like the creak of something massive and coordinated approaching, an expression of rhythm and collectivity as opposed to the late garrulity of individual con-flict of choice; and fear of being left behind.

But the human figure with the gun, after one brief uncertain look at the low sky now scored with a long straggling jet black frieze, returned his stare to the grey sliding surface of the water.

And then he must have thought for a moment the light had changed, darkened unaccountably. But there was no sun to be crossed by a cloud: no reason for a shadow moving the speed of the current, and with it.

He must have made out its size by the absence of eddies and scribbled currents . . . over a sudden whole area. And as it passed its edge showed as a shadow, an inch, about an inch and a half deep.

Perhaps fifty tons of ice. In one piece.

The geese came in four or five groups. They came perfectly.

He put up his gun in a loose and desultory way; and when the best—a perfect—moment came—did not fire.

He simply stood there. And the geese passed over.

Daylight soon showed his mouth to be so small and undeveloped, so anonymous in its lack of character as to suggest an organ that took in life by blind sucking. His eyes, on the other hand, were slightly protuberant, experienced without being intelligent. And the too numerous lines on his forehead and round the corners of his mouth were those of senility, yet had no pattern such as comes from a regular process like the kisses on St. Peter's toe, the waves on the sand or many years of ordered life sanctioned by custom, and similar people; by things visible and invisible. They were as ill-assorted as a burst of small fine scars from shrapnel. And indeed they seemed to have some affinity with the long smooth crease of an old wound on his left cheekbone; like little bum-boats round a liner.

He smoked another whole cigar at the wheel before starting the engine and while he smoked he stared straight ahead up the blank deserted track, stared through the shut-in smoke, and the raindrops which now gradually obscured vision, coming in rattling rushes on the roof and dribbling down the glass.

2

TWENTY TALL, crimson chairs like vacant thrones stood back, against the wall, from the long dining-room table. The twenty-first had been left askew, by a crumb-strewn plate, and the twenty-second was occupied by a man spreading marmalade, by feel, while his eyes pored sideways over the *Daily Express.*

"Alan," a woman's voice came clear down the passage.

"HALLO," he shouted with the loudness of protest.

She came and at the door said, "Alan."

He pored closer to the newsprint.

"Wot—for God's sake."

"John Harling's coming to lunch."

"Hurrah hurrah," he said absently: and then decided he meant it, after all, "Good."

Augustine Mackean was a type which is seldom given offence in a queue. She had thick raven hair and a relationship of eyes to nose-tip which was vulpine; and a deep, lusty body which to a small man might have suggested nothing less than a permanent physical rebuke. Her voice was quiet with everything in reserve; and her pale eyes, too, gave nothing away—not even to her husband. Genetically she was obviously nothing orthodox.

As now, she always seemed to be watching and listening, behind a veneer of studied indifference.

Before marriage Alan had hired successive big women for his pleasure; then marriage itself brought him his very blueprint of desire in this shape of "Tin"—who would inherit whole factories as well. For such a coup he had to thank partly his stately home and hence partly her mother, and partly, he rather fancied, himself. Tin had seemed not to figure in the transaction as a free agent until she got inside the house.

Since then she had sometimes made him feel, by comparison, a romantic. Which was quite a feat.

But they had never had any regrets—except the lack of an heir. And there was plenty of time for that. Meanwhile she left him in peace, ran things and had the kind of bottom he liked. In fact her moody body spoke to him, still, with an eloquence which made small beer of her words; made very pale ale indeed of the most amusing thing she had ever said.

"I suppose you know why he's coming," she said closer, and speaking with the quiet scorn which she had cultivated ever since marrying him.

"Because he wants a free lunch," said the laird, without censure.

"He's coming about Duncan's children."

"Then he's coming to the wrong house."

"About their education."

"I thought they were going to Lock Petrie."

This is a long cottage in the hills. He added with a touch of bleat: "State education's as good as anything now."

"He wants you to join with him and send them to a private school."

For the first time his concentration forsook the *Daily Express.* He took another bit of toast. "Well—he's mad then."

The Master of Mackean always spoke as though he had a cold. He never opened his mouth fully, just as he never held himself fully erect. With myopia, a partiality for rubber-shoes, big soft concealing chairs—the total effect was of almost hermetic escape and indifference—until his humour was touched—then in relief he opened up outwards, his eyes, his figure, and his mouth. Then only, he seemed to see things.

But when, as now, his cousin Duncan was the topic, he receded into himself more than for any other subject except his late celebrated father.

"What on earth have Duncan's children got to do with me?" he mumbled.

Merely because Duncan, an orphan, had been brought up here people still regarded the place as Duncan's home—as though he were a sort of younger brother. Or even an *older brother*. It may have been Puppa's secret wish that Duncan should be the heir— in which case it was just one more amazing instance of people's tendency to try and realise Puppa's dream world even when he wasn't there to direct operations.

"I thought I'd let you know," she said.

Something unspoken passed between them.

He got himself some more coffee.

"Thanks," he said stuffily, but with meaning. He took up again with the newsprint.

"And what about tonight?" she said.

"Well what about tonight?" Each interruption was becoming more painful. "I thought you said everything was laid on."

"It is. But you've bloody well got to be there."

"Okedoke," he said affably, hoping to reassure, and so dismiss her. "Is John staying?" Boredom was the enemy.

"He's sleeping at Duncan's so I suppose so."

"Goodo."

She said something else about being "On the dot" but the space-strip held him and he said: "Oh—right you are," with even more affability and cooperation.

At every estate dance his father used to welcome tenants as they arrived. But last year Alan had gone to a pub with a friend an hour before the dance started. The year before he had turned up only at midnight . . . from the parked cars with a half-bottle in his hand, had shouted up the steps "Ahoy" to the minister who was leaving.

He had in fact been mysteriously, almost ritualistically late for several local functions since his father's death.

Tin still stood there.

When he came to the end of the strip he felt obliged, in view of her continued presence, to make some finally reassuring reference to the dance.

He said, "Katherine's coming . . ." and he added diffidently, "to help."

But it was no good. He had—and he knew she knew it—merely listed a pleasure. The inconsecutive reference, his very physical stance, now, in that chair, made her more suspicious, minatory and cold.

He said, "Katherine's coming on from Granny to help," and he half turned to face her—which resulted in his protesting: "I'm not unpartial to old Kate—in small doses."

Tin was silent. He said—this time provocatively: "She knows the form," and he turned back, smoothed out a wrinkle in the rail-strike headline and cleared his nose harshly, expulsively, into thin air as much as to say: Now please, hop it.

"Nine P.M.," she said, because this could be good-bye for the day, for all she knew.

"Okedoke," he sang.

The noise of a car—swoosh—on the deep pebbles brought her face round slowly, like an animal sampling the air for danger.

"Oh God . . ." he said.

But she was already at the window, looking out, as she often did, as though the Communists Had Come.

Her capacity for silence when any normal person would have spoken sometimes came as near to gaining his attention as any-thing in which he had no vested interest ever did.

"Samuels," he stated.

She went out. "Who then?" he shouted after her.

The lack of reply did not long trouble him. He opened the *Daily Mail,* closed it and turned it round. His eye dropped to the bottom and for some minutes he pored over those other strips, going through them once quickly for the gist and a second time for detail.

The Austrian butler like a sad orangutan appeared with a tray and stood uncertainly by the door. Alan looked sideways at the carpet near his feet. "You can come back later," he said as though offended.

The man bowed gratefully.

Alan heard an unfamiliar male voice. He groaned, "Oh Christ," as though for serious physical pain.

Voices *approached.* Was Tin out of her mind?

He rose with bent head and took a hand, while mopping his mouth with his napkin, belching, making adenoidal noises of ambushed welcome and rebutting all suggestions that he had been disturbed eating breakfast.

"Not a bit," he muttered—and then raising his eyes to see how self-love would be received—whether by friend or enemy, he said affectionately: "I'm rather partial to a long lie."

So little did he open his mouth it sounded like "Nyong nie."

The man kept hold of his hand, and said nothing. A smart woman stood by him, smiling specially and anxiously.

Alan met the man's eyes, but not for long. One gaze like that and he knew.

Tin said: "Mr. Mackean . . . comes from Ontario."

A kinsman. He had thought it was to be the other kind of pilgrim: a Ypres salient man. About the time of the male change of life a Ypres salient man came and looked for Puppa—or since Puppa was dead—Puppa's house.

"Have you had breakfast?" Alan said reproachfully, but coaxingly at the floor by the man's shoes. "It wouldn't take my wife a minute . . ."

Tin cooked cold supper on Sundays which sometimes provided an idiom for the whole week.

His hand was still retained.

"Sir Alan," the man said—and Alan took in what might have been one of Puppa's keepers preserved in soap for ten years and then got up as a millionaire.

"Sir Alan, my wife and I never got to hear the news. Or we certainly never would . . ."

"What news?" Alan said tetchily.

Tin said with strong quietness: "Of your father . . ."

"That he died, you mean . . ." Alan stole another look—this

time of astonishment. The man in the moon must have heard of that death—page splash photographs, King and gillies behind the bier . . .

He said almost plaintively, "It's more than two years . . ."

Nobody spoke. Feet and silence: Alan had hated the first funeral. To have an additional memorial service thrust upon him during breakfast two years later was an act of aggression. He said speaking suddenly with the dignity of truth, to the man's feet, "He'd been very ill. He couldn't do the things he liked doing anymore . . ."

Alan again risked meeting the man's eyes—to see the effect of this comfort. God, he thought: We could have teased Puppa about this one.

"I've been living over in Europe, Sir Alan . . ."

"Yet," the wife interrupted, "there's plenty Mackeans back home. I don't see why some didn't write and say, George." She was agitated, for some reason horrified by their predicament.

The man let go of Alan's hand gradually. He said: "I've thought of Colin Mackean every day of my life."

Nobody said anything. Truly a muted bugle might have blown by a flag, half lowered. It was still like this. Driving Alan farther.

"Are you staying in the village," Tin said deflectively.

But the couple had raised their eyes to the height of the ceiling, the man cursorily, the woman dotingly, with her handbag at her navel.

Tin stood behind unaffected as always, but determined to see traditional-emotional capital kept strictly in gilt-edged, i.e., show round, even feed.

Alan seemed suddenly to say from memory a line of an obscure foreign book: "Mr. Mackean—it's very good of you to come. My father would have valued it. Greatly."

The Canadian had an odd face which didn't change.

Tin said: "Can you stay for lunch?"

Alan said: "You'd much better come to the dance. It's a rather grooling experience." And with a naughty myopic smile promising tradition and glee, he completed the camouflage of his swift reluctance to have them for lunch.

The husband walked through the group and out of it. "Permit me," he said with authority, and he went to the foot of Alan's father, done full length in kilt, velvet jacket and lace stock in the vivid alderman school of twentieth-century oils.

His silence as he stood beneath the picture isolated and relegated the group by the crumb-strewn plate.

Alan guardedly looked up at his father: luckily the painter had been clueless.

The almost deer-like softness of the dark eyes had been imitated; and the tragic, impersonal knit of the brows was something between the truth and a Horlicks strip-story advert. But simple people often supply with their wish and their memory the life that has eluded an artist.

The Canadian, clearly, had no objection.

He was seeing Colin, who used to stalk into a gathering, as three of them there remembered, with a flat smooth walk and his hands loose like weapons. The timbre of his voice was sensual; what he said sadly simple and objective. He was even sadly, simply, objectively facetious. Perhaps in his determination to do the things he had done, he had scorched, so to speak, too much personal earth. And so his face towards the end of his life had acquired the terrible dispassion of total self-discipline. Colin Mackean the idea had taken the place of Colin Mackean the man and to this transaction, during the Second War, illness and, worse, idleness, added the facial marks of martyrdom.

Most men had been a little afraid of him—in some forgotten part of themselves; and most women (in some often equally forgotten part) had wanted to go to bed with him.

Yet this vitality—which in his face took the form of an admitted capacity for evil, a proved capacity for violence made moving, made truly civilised a manner which in others would have passed for merely exceptional politeness.

Oh yes he was a hero, apart from the Victoria Cross, and by his lights had given his life daily domestically in order to save it. But what happened to his legend after he died . . . the legend of a man in whose hands a gear-lever or a copy of Marx (he had made himself handle both) were as literal fresh excrement in the hands of another.

When the Canadian turned round his face consorted less than ever with his bright prosperous city clothes and with the company. He looked anxious to say something. But not to them.

Alan said, "It's not too bad, considering."

"The last time I saw your father, sir," he said—making the word Sir now sound like an archaic courtesy—"was at a camp for blind ex-servicemen. When he'd made his speech—he said 'Gentlemen—I salute you . . .' and then he stepped back a pace and remained at the salute for a full minute in front of all those blind faces. I tell you—for a minute he gave them back their eyes. To weep with."

Alan had lit up a Dunhill, special blend. Perhaps this was the fortieth different account he'd heard of this occasion. He by now knew fragments of the speech by heart. Puppa had been a master tear-jerker——

"My father was a wonderful speaker," he mumbled.

Silence asserted itself like an intervening noise that made intercommunication an exhausting strain discouraging the sensitive.

The wife said: "I expect it's Sir Alan here in that photo you have, George. Why don't you show it?"

It took time to get out. Then Alan peered . . .

"No—that's Duncan. My cousin. I thought it would be. He used to live here. All the time."

The couple, confused, looked again, closely at the fourteen-year-old face ill exposed, in a bad light.

"You don't do much shooting then?" the man said awkwardly.

"I quite enjoy shooting pheasants and grouse—and duck if it's not too bloody."

Alan raised his eye, coolly, to the life-marked face of his remote kinsman: anything else?

And he had to smile, almost sleepily, and unconsciously to

moderate for his visitor the importance of it all.

"Is that right," the man said cryptically.

The couple took their leave, slowly, through the pictures, claymores and heads of slain beasts, stuffed birds in cages, and racks of archaic firearms; all paused instinctively by a moose, and peered beneath into the foggy ochre print of its first moment dead.

A moose: Canada. They talked.

At the top of the front steps the party had a bird's-eye view of a that year Packard.

Alan said: "You're not looking for a partner, are you, in Canada, Mr. Mackean?"

The man didn't know this sort of joke. His face assumed the doubting pain of the deaf.

Alan said: "Lovely then . . . tonight."

When they had gone: "Before my breakfast . . ."

"It was ten-thirty," Tin said. "Will you do the beer now?"

But Alan was rather pleased. He raised his eyes to the loch and for a moment came up the steps of this immense house and surprised himself at breakfast.

She had gone non-committally. So often her deeply fleshed back receded like this, using silence to suggest contempt—but he knew it was just a means of getting equal with him and his house —and his relations. She tried to imitate their kind of rudeness. Poor old Tin-Tin: she hadn't a clue.

"Open the beer," she said, receding.

He followed her in. "Poor chap. He's got it rather badly, hasn't he?"

She disappeared.

The complacence passed. He felt suddenly unappreciated.

Electric blankets on the beds where there had never been hot-water bottles, york ham where there had been cold carrion venison, wine where water, cars where crocks, amusement parks where "views," mechanised farms where weed patches, warmth where cold; no cousin Duncan where there had been cousin Duncan. Nothing but improvement. Yet people came eight thousand miles

to see where his father had lived, or they gave up coming eight
because he wasn't living there anymore.

The answer was an outsize gin-and-water.

As he passed, the telephone rang.

It stood white, accessible on a Peter Jones table, not hidden in
decaying mackintoshes. "Hallo——" he said high and weary,
because this morning was beginning to pile up on him.

"Alan?" curt and tough, one Mackean relation addressing
another.

"Duncan—what on earth d'you want?"

His cousin never communicated without wanting.

"D'you want Mary and me to come this evening?"

"You know you can come."

"Mary wanted to know."

"I'm quite sure she knew already."

The offensiveness was neutralised by custom: each to each.

"Alan, do you wish to hear something to your advantage? I've
got something to discuss. This morning."

"What . . . Well, I shall be at the Cass rifle range. You can come
there."

"Why?"

"I'm sieving the sand in the butts for lead. For my boat. Tootle-
oo."

"How about the geese?"

"What about the geese?"

"There's about four thousand. I let them go this morning. I
could have had several."

Duncan was always asking people to shoot geese, *his* geese, as
though the whole east-Scottish foreshore were his estate. He
particularly invited people he wanted "to see on an important
matter."

Alan said: "Herds of shore-shooters will be after them."

"Cock," Duncan said. "I thought you'd like a crack before
tonight."

Alan said nothing.

Duncan said: "Hallo. . . ? Unless of course you are required to be on the dot."

Silence.

"The tide is right."

". . . well O.K.," Alan mumbled. Then: "I may go down, I'll see. What on earth d'you want to see me about?"

"D'you want it broadcast?"

"O.K.," he mumbled. "Good-bye."

His slippers tripped and dragged on many carpets as he made his way to the lavatory. The *Daily Sketch* and new *Esquire* were by the gong, where he had parked them purposely, while ushering out the Canadian Mackeans. Forethought saved detours.

The telephone rang again. "Granny," he thought. He looked at his watch. 10.30: just after the Short Service.

He went through and locked the lavatory door.

After a time the Austrian came and reluctantly looking up, and round, at all the many doors picked up the receiver: "*Wass . . . wass,*" he whispered. "Go out, yeah. *Wass . . .* Hallo?"

The misshapen figure held the instrument from him like an animal upon whom a practical joke has been played. Dachau, a refugee camp and then this, bliss of bed linen, cream and money, dressed in tails. His stupor was metaphysical. He stood there faithfully holding out the plastic shape to the ancestors, the glimmering suns of swords, and the sheafs of spears. The silence towered above him, floor after deserted floor. The dead alien echoes—generations of voices, footsteps and doors slamming—oppressed him. He stood in a wreck at the bottom of the sea hearing voices. And so Clop—he put back the receiver and went away talking to himself a language he knew.

In the lavatory Alan thought of what he had arranged with sudden surprise like a person who has done a conjuring trick when he wasn't trying.

For it so happens, madam—he thought, I shall this year again be somewhat tardy for the ancestral beano.

3

TED DEAKIN, proprietor of the Mackean Arms, stepped in sneakers to the glass panel of the Private Lounge door. He looked in quietly and technically, like a gaoler.

Duncan Mackean surrounded by paper decorations and plastic Father Christmases was reading an old *Queen*. His stockinged feet were thrust towards the sunk Economy grate and he flipped through the pages jerkily as though at any moment he might discard the whole magazine with violence.

Deakin watched this dull sight for a whole half-minute and during this time the panel shed on the upper half of his face a visor of light from which his eyes looked out with cold impersonal understanding.

These eyes were white. They were like holes in something held up to sky, perhaps because it was sky which had made them white, years of brilliant brazen tropic skies, till the eyes had retreated, gathered about them delicate extra skin like a lizard's throat, and gone white and hard. Total suspicion too lay in these eyes.

But what was there to watch? Such passivity and slow relaxation —in a less bleached, a less defensive face—would have passed for pure interest. In his it looked like calculation.

For a year Deakin had taken Duncan Mackean's salmon for cash. Nothing written. Since then—like now—the little kilted Mackean had treated the hotel as a home from home, slumped down in it at odd hours and asked for drinks in a tone which said: Come on, turn an honest penny before you charge one.

Deakin gave him the drinks, and credit for petrol, and in the season continued to send him the hotel's overflow as lodgers: "for that mansion of yours." Sometimes he seemed to be taking a strange private payment just in watching Duncan as he did now. Making no pretence of having suddenly arrived, Deakin opened the door and said quietly: "It's Mr. Mackean . . ." and he smiled in a lipless way and with increased watchfulness as though to communicate had been a risk.

"The colonel!" Duncan said. "Come in, Colonel."

When Duncan spoke it was like the result of putting a penny into a slot. An incongruous clockwork event took place without change of the exterior. His tone was shrill and aggressive. His face remained set.

"Am I disturbing you?"

"Now, Deakin—don't stand there. Come in or go out."

The act—their double act continued.

Deakin had lived three years, now, in the legend of the uncle; and he had witnessed his funeral. In those three years he had got to know scarcely one native. Vaguely he put this down to the uncle —the stuff about the uncle. The sort of Tower of London stuff.

But he knew the son, Alan; and cousin Duncan.

Like all problems—which was the same as saying all economic problems—the legend required thought if it was to be solved. Deakin truly studied the Mackeans.

Duncan said: "I want a word with you, Colonel Deakin. Just sit down over there, will you."

The confidence of the act, the clear attack of the high-pitched voice brought a smile to Deakin's face. He said: "Reity-ho"— almost "Raity-how," because as Colonel-proprietor he had tortured his accent towards pure B.B.C.

He sat down, saying, "Isn't your lady-wife waiting for you?"

"Now just tell me in simple language, Deakin: how do you cook your books?"

Deakin smiled, rode the shock a moment and said softly: "Caught up with you?"

Duncan said: "Answer the question."

"What's the damage?" Deakin spoke quietly, with a hint, perhaps of help.

"I asked you a civil question. How do you cook your books? I expect a civil answer."

Deakin smiled: "Didn't I say they would?"

"Why haven't they caught up with you?"

Deakin enjoyed the moment.

"The trouble with your class is you want everything easy. If you want money you've got to apply yourself—work."

The word faltered on his lips. Duncan said:

"You've got to work, have you? Tell me more. Tell me more, Deakin. Is life what you put into it?"

Deakin's smile slowly disappeared.

"You owe me fifty quids' worth of meat, Mr. Mackean."

"The hinds are scarce this year."

"P'raps you've already shot your quota and the McNeill factor knows it."

"He can f—— himself."

There was silence. Then daintily, Deakin said, with his repressed accent lingering like a faint diaeresis on most vowels: "No no—you've got to apply yourself. You say things are worse. Perhaps they are: for your class. That's because you're learning the meaning of competition on equal terms."

The conversation seemed suddenly to bore Duncan. His eyelids lulled down as though he were going to close his eyes.

Deakin said: "Of course your upbringing was against you."

"What do you know about my upbringing?"

"Nowblesse owbleege."

"Come again."

"All that about your uncle."

"What about my uncle?"

"Bare feet on the hills—and sleeping in the people's cottages. Opposing the hydro-electric. Refusing to sell Loch Gannet to Butlins. I know it all. There's an old boy makes me sick with it. You can't put the clock back . . ."

"Oh, you can't put the clock back?"

"It was all right for him. Bloody good theatre. Living in a palace. Laying wreaths and making speeches. If I could make sure of my palace by sleeping every seventh day in fleas and bloody pigs I think I'd've done it. Shall I tell you what he was doing? *Scattering bread on the waters.*"

"Cock," said Duncan. "Bloody cock."

"And all that stuff about him going down the Gorbals in a top-hat, when he was a young man, just for the joy of a scrap. You can tell that to the Marines. If you ask me he got out at the right moment. Another year or two and he'd've found no one to be obleeged to him."

"I gather you knew my uncle pretty well, Deakin."

Deakin smiled slowly, grateful for the remark. He said: "I know his son—and his nephew. And d'you know what I know: they couldn't hold down a job—even in this state of full employment. *Any* job."

"Or d'you mean a wife, Colonel?"

Deakin had married an unattractive provincial heiress, twenty years younger than himself. He had divorced his first wife to do so.

He coloured faintly. "I'll tell you something else. Confidentially. The father couldn't have held a job either. Today. The great Colin Mackean couldn't either . . ."

He watched for the effect of this, beginning to smile, thinking Duncan was going to pretend not to have heard.

Duncan said: "Why don't you restrict your conversation to its natural limits?"

Deakin got up: "There's ten houses in this village take lodgers. I bet you're the only one that's going to pay the income tax a penny. And you're going to pay them three times what you owe them. D'you know why? Because you thought all that money—and more—*was yours by rights.* You resented even any discussion about it. Any forms. My dear Mr. Mackean, *nothing's* yours by rights. I learnt that when I was six. Shall I tell you what's yours? What you can get away with is yours. I'm surprised your uncle didn't keep you wise. He knew it O.K."

Duncan was in a slouched position, staring at the fire. He had the rather official look of someone who fears to let his face conform even approximately to his thoughts and feelings.

After a time this official face said unexpectedly and amiably: "Keep cool," and the edge of one deeply bitten thumb-nail stayed near his mouth. "I ask a perfectly normal question. I want advice. I want to know how you do your books. Just sit down here and tell me. That's all."

Duncan re-indicated the chair.

Without a sound Deakin reached the door. A maid came in with a brush. "Where are *you* going?" he said in his little countertenor's whisper, then, "Well, don't."

As she came back, and quickly, he gave her a kind of look in which his eyes seemed suddenly white hot.

This was not the discipline of the Catering Act; nor was the reaction merely that of an employee.

She did not look at him. None of the girls did. But they stayed on for years and were conspicuously well dressed. All were pretty till they got blowzy. Which was soon.

Voices sounded in the hall. Deakin paused and became still. He listened long enough to hear some words, the kind of voice: long enough it seemed to make sure it was safe.

Without a sound he went out, leaving the door open, as though on an empty room.

The decorations, the elongated concertinas of coloured paper over Duncan's head, were for a party which Deakin gave annually, free, to the children of the village.

When thanked he said nothing—only sometimes, if thanks persisted, he shook his head with a sort of incredulous indifference at the person's feet. And went by.

With children he was different.

4

By the front door of the former manse, above the loch-side road, a tall man got out of a car, and a passer-by might have been struck by his behaviour.

For this was no mere case of being a stranger. His expression, as he turned and looked down over the deserted loch, seemed to contain fear, fascination and revulsion.

Every harmless thing contributed: the Mackean Arms in the distance with three pumps like robots near the pier; the rhododendrons encroaching all round him on ill-kempt gravel; the jungle of larch, birch, and rowan giving place to dark cohorts of pine and above them the white snowy skin of immense hills mottled with thawed-out granite, scarp, and corrie; higher still white wilderness lost in cloud and everywhere the shabby thaw making the distance look like a confectioner's disaster. All contributed.

His car ticked with heat. He was cold and tired but his long, sensitive, would-be stern face at last grimaced slightly as though he had come six hundred miles to be played a huge metaphysical joke; to be put down where Social Man was not; where Time whispered Phoo in his ear. Beside Château Duncan.

"*Merde,*" murmured John Harling, and then as the door opened behind him, "*Mary!*"

He spoke his half-sister's name warmly and with a hint of penitence.

"How *very* nice . . ." he said kissing her.

And then he looked at her, into her, even as he was taking off his coat.

He was lanky and dark-chinned. His eyes varied, quickly and often, between the extremes of receptivity and preconception. He thought—visibly. And now after three years and much promotion with one of the serious weekly newspapers, a natural tendency to paternalism had increased, so that he bent towards almost everyone during conversation in an odd attitude of mingled patronage and humility.

It might be thought from his presence here, in mid-winter and during a rail-strike (and only two days before he was due at a conference in Geneva), that he was addicted to preserving family unity, that he was mother's boy getting together with father's girl, or something of that sort. In fact, John was proud of having "pulled up his roots," a procedure which he advocated, in occasional articles, to the whole nation. In fact, he had always regarded his sister's bitten fingernails, her often rumpled stockings, dresses of *gamine ingénue* and face which so many thought "angelic," all bore witness to some infantile taproot which she had failed to pull up. And now he had heard from a neighbour, and from his mother last summer, that Duncan was "killing Mary." He had heard she was doing the cooking, the children, the lodgers, the garden and the hens—the last three being the usual answers to "What does Duncan do now?"

"You look awfully well . . ." he suddenly insisted.

Often since he came back from the war, he had looked at her as he did now, trying to imagine that scene in 1943, seeing everything about her from complexion to expression, in terms of that moment. She had been thirteen. It was in the cottage they took, away from the blitz, in Berkshire. She had come in from school and found their mother had bungled suicide. No one else was in the house.

Mary herself had told him the story—with her permanent near-smile, which he had sometimes tracked to her blue eyes—and then to her mouth . . . her voice . . . her manner; without ever pinning it. When she spoke at length her head swayed infinitesimally as though she were slightly stunned: she had fetched

Don the blacksmith, she said . . .

Yes it would be "Don"—how well he remembered those odd alliances of hers; ever since she could walk.

"She was on the wrong bed with her skirt half off. She left a letter saying it was my fault."

She narrated her childhood freely, in the same way. Like a sort of ballad. Her face and voice were the jolly jerky metre, jolliest of all at last verses when psychological murder (John was sure) was announced in diguise . . . *Come up and see a surprise, dear, and all because of you.*

The various ballads had probably never been heard by anyone but him—least of all by Duncan.

Was that why he was here?

At the thought of Duncan, the expression of his work-worn, transparent face became such that she laughed at him as though unknown to himself a single redskin feather had been placed behind his ear.

"Have you swallowed something? Your nose is mottled. Are you perished? Or famished I mean. Or not. . . ?" and she laughed again.

"Or not!" he said.

"Oh dear: I've said it already. Do you still mind? And do I laugh too much? And too high. But 'or not' was the worst wasn't it?"

"Yes," he said and thought: because it ended in Duncan.

The month after he had been demobilised he had lived at home. They had breakfasted together in the dark dining-room in Lowndes Square. He had met her more or less for the first time— "Or not . . ." she kept qualifying every possible point of view with the possible superiority of its absolute possible—or more likely— opposite absolute. "Do you believe in God—or not?"

"Shall I marry Duncan—or not?" He had thought it wise to encourage her because Duncan, alone of all her hangers-on, wanted marriage and quick. The rest wanted to talk to her about God which somehow seemed to be themselves, until dawn.

Yes, Duncan was his too.

She said: "The wind will change . . ." and thus pointed the nearly lunatic length of time he had looked at her without speaking—though of course it was really only a few seconds.

"You look so well . . ." he repeated disingenuously, moving.

She said: "How was Glasgow?"

He frowned: "Mary—I *combined* it . . ."

"I merely meant: successful?"

"It was nothing . . ." He looked suddenly put out, almost past concentration. "I didn't have to go."

They went in.

"I didn't have to go," he repeated.

"Good."

In the passage he said: "Mary, was our mutual *mère* at all sufferable when she came?"

"She was rather sweet. I rather love her. Don't you? I mean, now."

Mary had the eyes of a child that had never seen a nasty thing. Their blueness burnt with a gay fixity which John put down sometimes to T.B. (she had been under observation), sometimes to "permanent mild hysteria," sometimes to the childish "taproot" already mentioned.

"She gave me the impression you were . . . dying."

"She loathes Duncan. Is that it?"

The chaotic remarks which streamed from her were like beads from dozens of broken, irreparable necklaces. She strung them in motley file on one precarious thread of irony, and then how curiously they contrasted with the constancy of her blue eyes. Yes —time surely stopped for her, he thought, long ago. By the toy-cupboard.

Suddenly, reminded by her eyes, he said: "Mary—I meant to write: what an extraordinary adventure that was. Your Glasgow hold-up . . ."

He sat down blindly in the unknown room.

"At the Blue Valhalla—the Blew Volhella," she added in Scots, "the man with the gun giving me my bag back . . . Wasn't it kind of him? The people at the next table were furious. A woman said he must be a friend. I was Questioned."

Silence.

"I see," he said fastidiously, and then with reluctant self-discipline, "I want to hear *everything.*"

But in fact he got up, and strayed round, away.

Obediently she was silent.

"It ended happily," he stated, and then turning to get a total view of the room: "Mary, how very nice." He had not expected to mean these words—and this detracted from their conviction.

The grey felt carpet with bright rugs on it, the coloured prints, the plain amber-coloured lamp shades and the orthodox long low stool before the fire, littered with periodicals, struck him as agreeable, prosperous and natural. He had no taste, he knew, but really, surely, this might have done for a *House and Garden* interior . . . That alabaster Greek-was-it vase there, in the oval alcove . . . and this, above, this miniature chandelier . . . with hundreds of glass pendants . . . It was all the sort of thing one saw . . . He had expected squalor.

"*Very* nice," he said again, this time achieving conviction and eliminating surprise. And he turned to look at Mary as though she were more and more a new person.

She had vanished.

An immense and prolonged hissing came through the open door. It died out suddenly. Her footsteps came fast and picking something up she said she was so sorry . . . Two toddlers whirled past her and in, and then stood still, gazing at their uncle.

"What. . . ?" she said, laughing. Then: ". . . my children," as though no one would ever believe it.

She was a mother.

Or not?

His face suggested not.

For again he was surprised. They looked clean, healthy and happy. He became avuncular, wrinkling the skin round his long nose, stooping to them as though he had much to learn from them, touching them gauchely. "My godchildren—Ronald . . . and Fiona. Excellent. Capital." Perhaps during that month, five years ago, his inability to think of his sister in terms of sexuality or maternity had been another reason for his match-making. And now in silence staring at the children he thought how right he had been. What*ever* else.

His stare now equalled theirs for relaxed passive curiosity. He became moved. Slight pepper behind the nose. He had to change the subject but made a certain point as he did so by putting his arm round his sister. "Good, Mary, good—I'm so glad." And then as he progressed through the furniture, examining the décor still further, "It *is* nice."

But she said non-committally: "Do you think so. . . ? Duncan does it all."

He stopped, still.

"Duncan . . ." The unexpected always disorganised him. Until reason and preconceptions had switched front, collated reports and published findings there was no government in his head to deal with. "*Duncan* . . ." he repeated, quieter but more intensely.

The house had changed.

From then on he went from room to room strangely.

The dining-room had yesterday's or were they last week's crumbs; marmalade with a spoon in it. There was a pram in the passage.

"He ought to be an interior decorator then. What's all this?"

They were at the door of a little room which smelt of turpentine and paint. "Of course—this is the Home Industry my mother mentioned . . ." he added staring in. "The lamp-shades."

"The lamp-shades," she said, showing him one.

"But *excellent* . . ." he said.

"We made two hundred pounds with them last year."

He fingered it uncertainly as though the fabric of his sister's marriage were beginning to slip from his competence.

"And you have a woman. . . ?" he said.

"Mrs. Barnes most mornings."

"And the lodgers, my mother said, brought in two hundred . . ." He was perplexed: "I mean, if my father gives you eight hundred a year, and you make four hundred yourself—and then the hens —I don't see . . ."

"What?"

"I mean you're flush," he said ironically, raising one lip slightly keeping it all light, a passing inquiry as he looked at a distant print framed in black and gold.

"The hen-man has to be paid."

"But Duncan does the hens."

"The hen-man."

"Then Duncan still has the netting . . ."

"That's finished."

"Then what does Duncan do. . . ?" He looked at her.

"What?" she laughed rather unnaturally and a timid look came into her face.

He repeated the question, and implied with his eyes that it was a simple one, for which laughter was out of place.

"What? Duncan's very busy. With small jobs . . . This place . . ."

He could not get the look in her face.

"But Mary," he said. "Things aren't too bad. I mean my mother painted a gruesome picture. Almost . . ."

He decided not to finish.

The children zoomed back and forth like bees round a flower, sometimes with minor destruction. She never addressed them, but sometimes touched them absent-mindedly, when they came close; without looking at them.

She said, "Isn't everyone broke? I mean except, you know . . . those people in cars you see."

"But with twelve hundred a year . . ."

"D'you want a statement of accounts? I'm frightfully efficient. Two hundred in rent to Alan, two hundred in cigars, two hundred on drink and one hundred in petrol—that makes, wait— seven. Two for income tax—nine—and . . . of course ten pounds on snuff . . . Snuff has gone up."

During this recital she fixed her brother with lively blue eyes which coupled with the jolly animation of her voice upset him more than he could say.

"Snuff . . . Cigars . . . ?" he said meekly. "Did you say . . . ?"

"Duncan likes the good ones. Two or three a day."

He said: "But three good cigars is one pound ten a day . . ."

"*Are*, dear, *are* one pound ten . . . One before breakfast, one . . ."

"*Before* breakfast . . ."

"In bed. John—would you mind frightfully if we continued in the kitchen?"

"*In bed* . . ."

He followed her in a stupefied way. She was clearly doing it on purpose.

Her blue, apparently blank and knowledgeless eyes had rested on him for a second, as she turned to go ahead.

"In *bed*, Mary . . . Don't you *mind*?"

His inclination had been to praise and approve everything; his purpose to pour cement indiscriminately over every expected fissure of the marriage. Now she had left him with the echo of his question which put simply amounted to "Do you mind your husband?"

He tried, standing in the passage, to phrase a general announcement that would make it mean something different.

"Mary . . ." he said, following.

They had reached the kitchen, and she passed through, in front.

His scrupulous, trim and slightly archaic suit, suggesting perhaps an editor of the *Manchester Guardian* 1910, or a family doctor in Shropshire 1950, was a pained brother of her slipshod jersey and deep dirty, flared corduroy skirt. Now his fastidious search for space to sit reflected his own neat bachelor flat.

"You're worse than Duncan," she laughed.

He did not know what she meant and lifted clear an armful of nappies, a teddy-bear, an egg whisk and one child's shoe. But where to put them? Was it wrong to wonder how to treat things which might have been assembled for a purpose, particularly when unwashed dishes, a library book, the *Radio Times,* a pile of mending and an alarm-clock disposed variously of space that would have been a solution?

"Why am I 'worse than Duncan'? I wish to sit down."

He was mildly offended. Presumably she felt guilty about the squalor and therefore had attacked his distaste which she had guessed. Dirty habits were usually nothing but poor health. He did not blame her for either but she must accept his squeamishness; and he would have liked to remind her some of the poorest people in the world managed to be the cleanest. He had often heard as much.

For a few minutes she was so much on the move that conversation was impossible, and he sat and wondered in what sense he could be "worse"—or rather—in any way the same as Duncan. After a bit he dismissed his fears as over-sensitive, and he looked edgily about him. This room was a different house. It suggested tattered underclothes beneath a smartish dress. Even a carton of groceries had not been unpacked. Perhaps they came days ago. And the sheets in the pram had been grey. He suspected dust everywhere.

Suddenly he felt Duncan *didn't come here.* Presumably that was what she had meant. His eyes followed her with less confidence.

She said: "You're lunching with Alan, aren't you?"

"Yes. But I very much want to see Duncan, and even more do I want to see you."

She said: "Duncan gets impossible if lunch is late."

A stout woman with a red face appeared. "I've put Jean in the pram, dear."

"Oh thank you, Mrs. Barnes."

"And I'll look in at two but I'll 'ave to floi now or Barnes'll create."

"Of course."

"And it'll be O.K. for tonight whatever he says."

Mrs. Barnes looked from Mary to her brother as though she'd like to say something. John rose. They shook hands. "She'll be pleased to see you," she suddenly said hotly.

He frowned and resumed his solemn position against the kitchen table.

"Mrs. Barnes is a sensationalist," Mary said. "It's the papers."

"Did you have burst pipes?" he said soberly.

"We had thirty degrees one night. Or was it ten?"

"Mary," he said, "do you get on with Tin better now?"

"Tin and I do the lamp-shades together."

"*Tin . . . ?*"

"It was her idea. To make two hundred pounds in cash like that is the equivalent for her of having another two hundred and sixty thousand pounds invested. She showed me on a bit of paper."

He hooted once in an ill kind of way. And then because Mary had not spoken ironically or satirically he stared at her in disbelief. This was another ballad.

"She always comes here. She won't do it at Ardriach." Mary looked at him: what did her smile mean?

"Well, good," he said uneasily. "Very good. I've never made anything . . . like that."

She moved, she stirred, she clattered objects, neatly like a demonstration gun-crew, and was tripped repeatedly without falling.

"We admire your articles," she said in mid-exertion.

"Thank you." After a moment he said: "I mean, where's Duncan *now,* for instance."

"He went after geese. Do you think shooting beastly? I adore meat."

"Geese . . . oh yes," he said suddenly, as though he had never doubted. "I see. But I mean *what does he do most days—all day?*"

"What?"

Was she deaf?

"Very well," he said sadly. "As you like."

He turned from her silence. He looked out of the window at

the desolate view and thought of waking up in the smog of Duncan's cigar.

His question hung in the air about them both, and soon he listened to her very movements as though they could teach him if he listened right.

Suddenly she said: "I don't know."

And that was just what he had dreaded. Not the substance of her reply but the tone. He had begun to suspect the substance—but he had prayed that she might speak it with disciplined resignation, or with irony, or even with faced fear (another ballad), or frivolously—but not, oh not, as had happened, suddenly *differently* like a child getting stuck in lines to be learnt by heart. She didn't know. Mightn't he see in her absolutely blue eyes now a question to *him:* what *does* Duncan do all day? Her back was towards him.

Minutes passed.

"Mary . . ." he said. "*What happened* when my father offered Duncan the job with the Edinburgh bank? I got the impression he only had to turn up on time to be earning two thousand a year by now."

She said: "It is Written 'I want No black-beetles at my funeral.' Colin's will."

"Black-beetles . . . ?" his voice was blank.

"Bankers, i.e., you, dear—in a larger sense. White collar. Bourgeois."

After a moment he said: "The Mackeans are very stupid, aren't they? I mean *really* stupid."

She looked frightened by the word. "Stupid . . ." she said, "Are they stupid?" Then: "Would you have called Colin stupid? Did you know: he adored me. And he couldn't bear Tin. That was the trouble, at first. But after he died and she had kept us in the garage flat in the dark for a year she forgave me. I'm O.K. now."

"*Laissons-là,* for the minute, Colin's enlightened discrimination between you and Tin . . ."

"Don't be beastly now."

". . . aren't the others really stupid?"

"But I'm stupid." With this utterance her minute swaying of the head became pronounced.

"I see . . ." he said gravely; and clinically.

"I loved Colin."

"He was a sort of archetypal Highland god-figure, wasn't he?"

"He was sweet. He made me laugh. The people here would put their hand in the fire for him. Shall we try? With a brazier? This afternoon. I've always wondered if I could—for anything. Wouldn't you like to be able to—for something?"

She laughed at his expression.

"You *do* look extremely well, Mary."

"Good. Have you come to be kind? Thanks frightfully for the offer of education. I mean really. Duncan's determined Ronald should go to Eton. He'll go straight from D, isn't it, to National Assistance. That's where Duncan got. D. But he's quite right. I mean a room of your own: . . . or not. I mean: now I simply don't know. Anyhow: thank you, John. Should I have said it ages ago. I suppose I should. It all seems so strange. In the circs. You here . . ."

She looked up at him—blank, knowledgeless . . .

The noise of a car approaching came from the front of the house.

She paused in what she was doing and then resumed strenuously, saying, ". . . I was so pleased to see you."

The continued non-committalness of her blue eyes, even as she said this, moved him. He didn't know why. He rose and took her shoulders.

"I was, honestly," she said impulsively, as though as a result of his touch. She added: "I think I was meant to tell you something. But I forgot."

She became quite still. A door slammed in the distance. Then she said: "Yes. It's gone."

5

A SHADOW welled up in the passage checking John. It became a big
dog as it crossed into the half-light of the main passage. There was
something wrong with its coat. It gave a mournful half stifled bark
and stood as though still only half convinced that the moment to
wake up and live had come.

"Well, Harling—what brings you here."

He spoke from near the front door, down twenty feet of passage
and his tone seriously questioned John's presence as though no
correspondence arranging this moment had ever passed between
them.

"You did expect me . . ." John said, taking in the waders, the
whole mid-morning effect with astonishment.

The silhouette fended off the dog until it made him stagger.
Then there was a rush of shrill Gaelic and the animal cowered as
though struck.

"As long as you don't stay too long. Tell me—as a friend: why
do you write such cock on Wednesdays? All that crap about the
big Four, 'Although Mr. Molotov's present attitude to free
German elections represents a palpable advance on Torquay and a
noted step forward from Mr. Vyshinsky in New York, it yet
remains to be deducted' . . . I could do that."

"Well why don't you?"

"I happen to see that sort of stuff exactly as Mr. Bulganin sees
it. But you're excused, you do it for money."

"Why don't you do it then . . . ?" It really was absurd this: he
couldn't yet see the man's face.

"Shall I tell you? Because I've got my self-respect to consider; also respect for the public. Both the one and the other, Harling, would be prohibitive. Have a drink. Are you lunching with my cousin? You might tell him from me that he is known at the hydro camp as Seretse." He sniffed. " 'Seretse Rubberbum' to be exact."

They moved into the living-room.

He strutted over to the drinks and poured out two quarter tumblers of whisky. John laughed, then suddenly stared, like a specialist. Under that gaze the visor of Duncan's little armour was raised and two . . . remote eyes met his.

"Christ, what's the matter with you—don't you like whisky? Hm?"

The little grunt at the end was loud.

Then he said, "In a moment I've got two guests coming. Two Mackeans from Canada."

He took up a position centrally before the fire, legs apart, swirled his whisky two or three times and then "knocked it back." His reticence on the subject of his guests gave a dignified inkling of his responsibilities towards them.

"Friends?"

"Any Mackean is a friend, Harling."

"Good . . ." This was a dream. John waited for the next word without a clue as to what it would be.

A car turned into the gate at the bottom of the short drive. Duncan eyed it like a Governor-General who bears his social cross with a good grace.

He said: "You'll have to excuse me. You've chosen rather an unlucky day. After this I've got my cousin, Seretse . . ."

"Well, I'm sure we can talk later."

Duncan paused beside John and taking his arm above the elbow, like a dancing master, he looked down at his feet. "How's the leg, John?"

Two years ago John had had a mild attack of polio. He now moved the affected foot freely off the ground, as a reflex to the *genuine paternal* consideration in Duncan's voice. "It's O.K.—

quite O.K. now thank you," and he added sincerely, "I very much appreciated your letter at the time . . . I did, Duncan. It arrived . . . on the right day." Yes indeed. Exactly right, he thought, reviving in memory his incredulity, at the phrasing, the timing, apter both than any other letter, "I was having a fright," he said reflectively.

"As long as the movement has come back a hundred percent," Duncan said. "Even though you're not exactly an athlete . . ." He began to move again. "We meet tonight I suspect—chez Seretse."

"But Duncan—when do we talk? . . . *Duncan* . . ."

Duncan stopped near the door. A side window gave a view of the main road and the loch's edge through sub-tropical foliage. At this moment a big lorry, loaded with sacks, like a vast moving mound, crossed the gap. The size, the nearness and yet the silence, for a moment brought home the thickness of the windows, fitted double against winds.

Duncan's interest in the movement, his whole stillness drew from John instinctively the repetition of his name: "*Duncan* . . ."

The sill buzzed low. John said above it: "I'm sure we could fit something in."

Duncan stirred and said mechanically: "Well I'm not."

"Duncan, I came six hundred miles to discuss . . . the covenant for your children. It's to be presumed you'll grant me an interview."

The little man's manner, his stance, his very atmosphere so absolutely excluded the idea of obligation to John that for a moment John wondered if he had imagined their formal and courteous correspondence on the subject of educational covenants. Duncan's letter style and handwriting had been a weird cross between Lord Macaulay and a Bond Street hatter.

John smiled pleasantly—even appreciatively. But could the joke now end?

Duncan said: "Hasn't the *much* spoken to you? I gave her clear instructions. About that and other relevant matters."

"The *much* . . . ?"

"Mary *much* . . ." he said going out. "*Much:* a donkey, or moke,

Harling. She has my instructions."

Suddenly he paused. "Aren't you lunching at Ardriach?" There was an odd note in his voice as he mentioned his former home. John said he was.

"I suppose you're spending the night there?"

"Duncan . . . I asked in my letter if I could sleep *here*. I'm only *lunching* at Ardriach to discuss the matter which you seem so reluctant, now, even to mention."

"So you're not sleeping there . . . hm?"

John could scarcely believe his ears: the man was relieved! His voice had lifted, brightened, and he faced John. Was the place his mistress?

"They didn't offer you a bed? Hm?"

John made an impatient gesture.

"I don't understand . . . But Duncan—before you go . . . May I point out . . . I've got to get back to London tomorrow. And tonight, we dance. But this afternoon . . . tea. How about tea . . . here . . . ?"

Duncan said: "Why don't you stay longer? Shall I tell you what coming all this way for thirty-six hours is? Neurotic, psychoneurotic, Harling," and he moved off, with his thumbs in kilt waist, followed by the dog whose chin nearly rested on his shoulder.

Suddenly he stopped. Where he stopped, the light caught the side of his face so that the long deep scar played a trick. His near eye stood out too far above the wasted flesh. John remembered war-burns which pulped all facial lineaments of personality; and then were supplanted at last by "new faces"—sometimes more terrible than any jungle mask even though smooth and proportionate. Now for a single second as Duncan stood with a "new face," John felt a twinge, as though his own personality, his identity too, had become as doffable as clothes, and that once doffed he would have to come to terms with . . . that trick, there, of light. For that was all it was, he now saw, as Duncan moved a step farther.

But for some reason he remained chilled and upset.

He called: "You still haven't answered my question . . . I think
we *should* talk. You see you still haven't really convinced me it's a
good thing for your son to go to Eton."

"What!" Duncan said blankly.

"To Eton was what I said."

"I don't get you."

John gathered himself, for he was dealing with a pachyderm:
"Because weren't you yourself miserable there; and wouldn't
your uncle quite simply have run away at sixteen . . ." and then
("black-beetle" had jarred) he added, laughing, surely as the
Mackeans liked, "and wouldn't your great-grandfather have
decorated his room not with caps, boy pinups and pop-canes—but
the lites of the headmaster—or perhaps his head mounted, in a
mortar-board and judges' tabs. Duncan . . . Perhaps you ought to
consider your children's background more subtly before throwing
them in with an economic group they probably won't be able to
stay with. There is either the past or the future. Preferably the
latter. But I don't see that in your children's case Eton is a good
psychological investment for either. Could they earn a living by
the humanities, then *perhaps* . . ."

Duncan turned. His face was vacant. "Humanities, eh? Have
you a glossary? When you marry, Harling—marry a glossary. I
believe in complementary marriages."

Then he said: "Don't give me theory. It's all cock," and he
went.

In the kitchen Mary said: "How d'you find his lordship . . . ?"
She caught John's eye as she passed from cooker to shelf.

He said thoughtfully: "Some Canadians, Mackeans, have
come . . ."

Now she avoided his look.

John said: "One wonders why . . ."

"It's quite above board."

"Well I didn't suggest . . ."

"He'll show them the famous mace . . ." He stared. "Didn't
you know? It has blood and hairs from the first war. I thought

everyone knew about the mace. Colin left his war things to Duncan. Some of the people who come remember the mace. It's in a room here."

She lived with an implement clothed with human blood: a tangible boast that killing had been both effective and enjoyed. She allowed it. He simply stared at her.

"A mace," she said—in her ballad style.

"I see . . ." Then at last he said, "Mary—when Duncan arrived you were saying there was something you were meant to tell me. Now Duncan says the same. What did you mean?"

But the visiting Canadians seemed to have affected her. She talked on, fast:

"And his scrapbook. He's got a wonderful scrapbook. Cuttings, about Colin, and ops. Do you like cuttings about ops? And Arnhem. And bits out of the *Daily Mirror* and the *People* about class warfare, Guards Officer Drunk. He cuts it out. Then on the next page you find a bit copied from a book by a guardsman: 'Our officers, with a few exceptions'—as there will always be"—she added with talented sententiousness—" 'were first-class chaps.' " She laughed. Her head swaying. Was he being teased? She must have sensed how alien it all was to him.

"Mary, I asked a question."

She looked at him with that stunned note in her blue eyes: everything funny. Everything, everything.

She's a child, he thought. None of it is real to her.

"Am I hiding things?" she asked, apparently, herself.

"Mary—why does Duncan refuse to see me?"

"Listen!"

They heard voices. "He's busy. That's all."

Some minutes passed while he watched her work.

"I'm so sorry," she said incoherently. "Am I nuts? Are you bored?"

Then his offers of assistance were kindly rejected on the grounds of his probable incompetence. Other things apart he felt unhappy—because unfunctional.

Suddenly he said: "That filigree chain round your neck . . . does it end in a crucifix?"

Her face at once became crimson—so much so that he too became embarrassed. Because why blush? A funny distorted smile came on to her face and she touched it as though confirming its presence.

"Well . . . ?" she said.

He had a horror of personal remarks. He was ashamed. "Forgive me: it was—abstract really—a person who isn't a Catholic. Or are you now?"

"No."

"No—then I just wondered . . . But nothing. Or rather. Good. There's nothing to be ashamed of."

"Ashamed . . ." she looked oddly at him.

Then he said: "What's happened to that priest who used to write to you every day?"

"Father Appleby . . . He does a Loch walking tour each year. He stays a night."

"You mean he now comes *north* to see you." It was incredible. He closed his eyes a moment and then muttered: "I find it mildly obscene."

She said defensively: "You look rather like him sitting in that chair. Venerable, solicitous and old-fashioned . . . What's wrong . . . ? He's sweet. Last time, just at this table, where we'd had supper he suddenly said to Duncan: Would you mind, Duncan, if we all said a prayer. To Duncan. And we did."

John said liberally: "I suppose that could only have been a good thing."

"But I mean wasn't it odd? In a house. Suddenly. And the way he said 'Duncan.' "

"How did he say 'Duncan'?"

"As though he had known him for ages."

"Well—that's what they should do," John said professionally.

"You don't think it was odd. I suppose he does it everywhere . . ."

"I expect so."

What was she talking about? He stared at her and then felt he had informed her on a subject of which he was entirely ignorant. This, he now remembered, she often made people do.

The noise came of a car departing.

"Wouldn't you like to see the mace?"

He made a half-hearted gesture. Was she serious? Why was she anxious to show him? He would take her word. He simply didn't see the point.

"I think you *should*. But I must finish this."

In a few minutes they went out into the passage.

"Duncan . . ." she called. "Duncan . . . I thought I heard him go upstairs."

"I heard someone go up."

"He probably went to change . . ."

The big retriever slumped in the passage, looked up at them dully. She looked down.

"He's gone," she laughed.

John came to her side. He looked at her, fearing he should see in her face something underlying the bright tone, something to do with Duncan having come and gone without a word to her. But she showed no sign.

He peered ahead through the Gothic windows of the porch. The rhododendrons were moving restlessly in the wind which soughed under some door nearby. There was still snow on the leaves.

"But where?" he said dyspeptically.

She laughed at his tone which suggested that here there was nowhere to go.

She went in to her left. "Well . . . Perhaps you should take off your shoes. Tread softly, for you tread on his dreams . . ."

He understood so little that he looked at her with concern. She was talking so wildly.

"Let them as arn't s' tall stand in front. Now . . ."

"Mary. Be yourself. There's no need to be someone else . . ."

The darkness, the smell, Duncan had upset him. He squeezed her arm, penitently, at once. But she could hardly go on: "Well here we are (is that better?) and there's the famous mace. That's not ink. It isn't dried ink—or old grape skins—or rust—it's human blood, and hair. Look at that hair there. That one. Perhaps from Bavaria, Prussia, Vienna. I often wonder what the owner looked like . . ."

"That's unnecessary."

"Well, that's the mace. His best day was seven. Those are all German arms and gadgets. That's Turkish—for torturing."

"I see."

"And here's the scrapbook—'Come on, Margaret—make up your mind'—I didn't know that was here. He keeps it up to date. But it goes back—'Laird said No to £1 M.' 'Blinds drawn in lochside hamlet.' 'King at mountain grave.' "

He said: "I can read." This time he could not even apologise to her, or look at her.

He peered reluctantly as though to read a letter left lying about: Duncan's *Livre d'Or*. His lips parted in clinical fascination. He always kept moving, as though merely "looking in" on it all.

There was a faded sweet smell of cigar smoke and mustiness. The plush grip of a heavy sword was mouldering and a stuffed eagle suffering a dead death by leprosy.

She was silent, over the book.

"Why did we come?" she suddenly said quietly and simply. "You're asking me . . . ?"

A photograph of Colin Mackean in a war setting, 1916, was so similar in dress, ambience and equipment to a photograph of him in Scotland, 1928, that John's interest mastered his scruples. He peered closer. Even the expression on the worn swarthy face and the muscling of the trim little body bore witness in each case to humorous, self-infliction of moral and physical ordeal. Surely there was a mistake: pine stumps and shattered trees, common to each scene. He asked if there had been shell-fire in Scotland in 1928. Mary said there had been an extraordinary storm.

"And he took part in it?"

"He tidied up."

"And there's your hold-up," John said amazed. "There's you . . . I just saw the *Telegraph*."

"That's the *Daily*——"

"GUNMAN GALLANT—(TO ONE)" in huge capitals. The italic caption said: "You *can* take it with you."

She said: "Duncan thought we might get damages."

"But there was no joy . . . ?" John was suddenly a dry astringent gunman to save himself by inoculation from this unbelievable proximity to the genuine article.

"Absolutely none."

To spare himself saying anything he pored over the newsprint, prey to many conflicting sensations. "Do you often go to . . . that sort of place?" he said at last.

"It wasn't on the menu."

"No . . . no. But I mean the woman, accusing you of being the gunman's friend."

"Isn't she everywhere?"

"I don't know. Is she . . . Perhaps."

He stood up and looked round again, with greater uneasiness.

"He's gone to see Alan, I think," she said.

He turned surprised eyes on her and at last said:

"Yes: he said he was going to see Alan."

And for several seconds they remained in silence.

It was dark.

She looked up at a banner, threadbare as a pest-stricken leaf.

He looked round with a sense of space and time which the darkness increased, as though the wooden door of a strange cathedral had closed behind him. Colin Mackean. He raised his eyes, as it were, involuntarily to the roof of this alien, in his time famous, gentle killer and loved administrator. All this, he felt with a sudden *frisson* looking at the objects, had not been in the name of vanity.

"Well, that's all over," he said. "We've got to vomit up the past."

"Have we?" She was acting, he thought. Or teasing. He would

do her the credit of pretending she hadn't spoken. "That would leave the present," she said. "And a sort of stump."

In the passage he said: "Perhaps Duncan's right: there's nothing to discuss. Nothing you and I can't fix."

"Oh no," she said. "See Duncan. You must see Duncan," and then as thought she had spoken too keenly—"I mean: why not."

"Are you educating me? First the mace; then Duncan."

She blushed. Her head swayed dizzier than usual and suddenly her lips trembled while her eyes shone with that huge irrelevant happiness that fed them.

"I'm sorry, Mary." And he was.

He took her arm. She freed herself weakly.

"Won't you have to go soon? Come back afterwards. You'll find Duncan. You can be alone—*à deux*—*tête-à-tête*. Tin and I will be painting in here."

"Today . . . But couldn't you have said you can't, today?"

"Oh no," she said. "No no no. I couldn't."

"But . . . why?"

What was there so funny about him, about almost everything he said—so that it seemed she had moments of difficulty in restraining herself from the most abandoned laughter.

"You don't understand. Tin would mind. It's her favourite afternoon. The painting afternoon."

"But just *today* . . ."

She stared, stared smiling. "They're frightfully good to us."

A child began bleating beyond the porch, and the telephone rang.

He went into the living-room while she turned to the instrument.

She came back carrying the child. "That was 'Granny' Lefevre. She's ninety-four. She knew you were here. She rings up all day. All the family. Even in London. But she just rings here when Duncan's out. And she asks where he is. She pretends the interest is me, but it's really him . . ."

As Mary said this her eyes rested on John with a strange dewy brilliance. She might have just finished laughing a long time—or she might have been about to cry . . . or to "tell him all" . . .

"What is it . . . ?" he suddenly said vaguely.

She sat with the child. "There—there's uncle. Duncan told me you wrote to his commanding officer for a sort of reference when he was courting me . . ." Her eyes smiled all the time. It was all happy.

He looked amazed and then ashamed but raised a finger of protest: because put like that . . .

"But now you feel guilty for encouraging me to marry him, don't you? I believe that's why you're here. Well, you needn't—I love Duncan." And she said this only as though concerned for John's comfort.

"Of course you do," he said frantically.

"Surely you understand that. Even if old Mrs. Lefevre doesn't."

"I never said . . ." His finger was still up: everything was being *put* in the wrong way. "I never suggested you didn't."

How had it all begun? He scarcely knew what had been said. There was no argument—no next step for words. He tried to clear himself of having thought ill of Duncan, of having pitied her. He simply did not know Duncan; and if, still, he were incapable of meeting her without feeling pity, was he unique in that? She could not travel without being adopted by a porter, or shop without getting preference. Let her admit it. She was a child.

Calmingly and normally he said: "Mary, it's getting late. I'd better go. I don't know the way."

He had intended to ask how he could meet Duncan in the afternoon but after looking at her for a moment merely said: "I'll come back afterwards."

She smiled at him then as much as to say it was he, not she, who concealed things, and wanted the impossible.

6

THE Cass Rifle Range is now derelict. Even the large, finished formal excresence on the horizon, the butts, are beginning to look like any of the surrounding dunes.

Mackean's Volunteers (for the Boer War) were cradled here. They became coast Regt. (T.A.) for the peace, then Seaforth for Flanders, and T.A. for the next peace and then Seaforth for the desert. They usually had a Mackean in command. With them Brazilians, Negroes, Mohammedans, Poles, R.A.F. Regt., and Home Guard had here marked the prime of the .303 rifle and the old age of British power.

Now the graduated firing points, shallow dais of cut sea-turf are beginning to revert to sand, warren, constellations of thyme and tufts of spiny, tubular grass.

From the eight-hundred yard mark to the butts was only a small inch of the space available.

Close, on the sea side, the dunes sheered off into sky like an edge of the world; on the other sides, and inland, the flat waste sank with the earth's curve before the hills rose.

In such a place the clouds laid claim to the eye with a variety the ground lacked, and today the course of rain-storms could be marked—long trailing opacities like grey jelly-fishes; and the low sun was busy, bowling along through fast scud or, far inland, penetrating a solid grey floor with one tremendous, still sweep of light.

The wind moved the wasted tips of the dune grass and

emphasised the isolation of the single figure by surrounding it with a stir that was not alive.

There was no sound anywhere. Only once the long belated howl of a jet crossed silence as settled as a Buddha's smile.

The figure had three trophies from the tide-line—stake, green glass ball and kettle without hole. It crossed the raised edge of the dunes and moved towards the butts, beside which was parked a new purple Jaguar.

Alan walked as slow as a woman along a store counter, his eyes roving at his feet.

He packed the trophies shipshape in the boot and took out a sack, spade, fork and earth-sieve.

For an hour he dug, humming peacefully and repetitively, forked and sifted in the butts bank and had assembled two and a quarter pounds of nickel-plated lead rifle bullets when Duncan's Hudson came lurching up and parked beside the Jaguar.

Neither within nor without did he react. He worked till Duncan's feet cut into the very target for his next dig.

"Well, what can I do for you, Cousin," he said, with the minimum articulation. "You're standing on a very likely spot. Robertson says you took the old potato lifter."

"I salvaged it. Is that what he means?"

"Well, bloody well bring it back. We still use it."

"I haven't finished lifting."

"They'll be mud by now, old fruit. Why can't you ask . . ."

"Robertson would have said no."

"Why?"

Silence. Then Duncan said:

"Because he knows I know why Struie doesn't make a profit."

Alan dug a bit.

"Robertson doesn't fiddle any more than's normal nowadays."

Duncan was now sprucely dressed in the style of a laird at an agricultural show. He had a suitable tweed jacket with stags-horn buttons, a mature, faded sporran and discreetly shabby kilt, watch chain and brogues with immense black tongues that folded back almost to the toes. He stood as though on a public platform, half turned towards the proximity of manual labour. Or like the statue-stance of a leader.

Once when his father was carrying more Blue Hares down the hill than the keepers, Alan had raised a single stoat from his trouser-pocket and striking just such a stance, had proclaimed to some appreciative debs, "If Puppa would only realise it, I'm a sort of Garibaldi." But such nuances had been lost on the family. He had finally felt almost parental, forgiving, for that famous man's inability to address him except in tones of reluctant resignation; forgiving; even for the entailing of every bloody stick on to his, Alan's, hypothetical son, or—should he not produce one—on to "Duncan my nephew, and his heirs and successors." Yes, he saw his father's point of view (God knows, it was as big as Ben Slear), but with his cousin—with that stance . . . (Alan drove the spade in hard) . . . a saint would fail to have a relationship.

The trouble was Puppa had created a little religion which began with the words—I believe in myself, alias Loch Slean, alias the people round about; alias also forests, fighting, the future and Duncan my nephew. Even in Puppa's day to put across the credo had required a straight left like a horse's kick, a gift with people which the couch trade could envy, a jolly old ace of spades under his kilt—and the First and Great War. Duncan only had the Second Great War which was chalk from cheese, but he had carried on the credo with certain weird embellishments such as taking snuff, and standing like this. As a result he was crippled not only with feelings of inferiority towards the world, which may have been Puppa's trouble too (concealed under a bloody great arc de triomphe), but also towards the credo, towards Puppa. This last was going to require some fixing.

He sniffed and dug, beside the alien foot.

After what happened last summer (the thought came like a gift —but suddenly and disingenuously) he took it he could be excused from making the smallest effort. He blinked and sniffed evasively, said "Goodo" to a glint in the sand and was glad to change the subject—i.e., Duncan's purpose, whatever that might be—for this sudden rescuing memory of last summer: a killer for almost anything Duncan could say.

In fact it was months since he had thought about it but now with every silent second that passed it became more and more his cross which he had humped through the months thus far, but perhaps no further.

"Your foot . . . thank you."

"He sells spuds at two bob under price all round."

"Oh, not Robertson still?" Alan bleated.

But he did not help him to another subject. Nor would he say: What do you want? The fact that Duncan had come twenty miles to ask for something (no other purpose was conceivable)—and yet stood unable to bring out anything except how much Robertson fiddled struck Alan as an extension of his cousin's perennial stew, which being of his own making, he could stay in, stew in as long as he liked, provided he didn't continue to straddle with his ludicrous brogues a quite exceptional seam of spent W.D. lead.

"Would you move, please . . . ?"

But as time passed, the silence became oppressive. He began to wish Duncan would go away. Something about his mere presence began to get on his nerves, perhaps because such a rendezvous had never happened before. In the past Duncan's pleas had been disguised as "suggestions" served up as matey taunts. And the meeting places had been—or seemed—fortuitous.

Suddenly, into the short foggy field of Alan's view, as he stooped by the spade edge, another hand appeared by his. Duncan was helping him.

"What are you doing?"

"Well—do you want all this tin or not?"

Alan muttered thanks. But after five minutes of seeing his cousin's hand sifting beside his own he said in his most mouth-shut inarticulate wordy and self-conscious manner: "Possibly we should dispense with business. Probably you want to get back."

And then he said: "Duncan, old fruit. Perhaps I should warn you—if this is a touch, it hasn't got an earthly. Not after last summer."

Duncan's back was now half to Alan.

"Wah . . . ?" he said. "A touch . . . ? What d'you mean a touch?"

He sounded astonished and slightly indignant; yet the next thing he said was: "I owe money."

"Oh Christ . . ." Alan groaned.

Responsibility of any kind was as easy for his reflex nervous system as eating dung; but responsibility for Duncan defied image in the concrete world. For about fifteen years he had been conditioned, as a hen is conditioned to the noise of the bucket, to the idea that Duncan would one day have to be virtually responsible for the name Mackean—even without the perks—and therefore, *for him.* Nothing now could perhaps reverse the sound of that particular bucket.

"Well, if you got a regular job you could pay it back," Alan mumbled.

"That's what I thought."

Alan had known Duncan's voice all his life; but this was not it; nor was this the sort of thing Duncan said. And so he did not answer at once.

"Well, get a job then," he said uneasily, and began digging again.

"What about one of the farms?" Duncan said.

"*What* about them?"

"You've got three in hand."

"Oh God, Duncan. When you can keep a pig-man for more than a week, come and ask me for a farm. At least don't."

"Well then I'll ask you now. The only time I ever lost a pig-man was when you took him with higher wages."

Alan dug.

Duncan said: "The Tax people have stung me for six hundred. By March one."

Alan rested again without looking at his cousin. What else; just what else?

He did not suppose Duncan had the smallest idea what he would do next. If he didn't get the money, he would apply to the Harlings—and then to some uncles.

It wasn't, he told himself, as he blew his nose which didn't need blowing, that this would be the last of it.

He sniffed and made faces, putting away his handkerchief; this would be the beginning. It wasn't as if paying off the debts would make any difference. It would just be throwing good money after bad. Sooner or later Duncan must face up to reality. Procrastination merely magnified the day of reckoning. Duncan must grow up.

The clichés fitted so well that Alan—with a certain diffidence about their not bearing his own customary trademark—decided to deliver them.

He did so in a bumbling querulous voice interspersed with the clink of metal as a bullet went into the sack. The quite exceptional view, of five distant hillsides matted with his almost mature timber, worth about six hundred thousand pounds, did not consciously occur to him as being visible to his cousin. He ended sincerely: "Any fool can make money today. All you need to do is get up slightly earlier in the morning—and fluff to some under-current of popular need or wish like fish and chips or comics. And then pull your finger out."

His articulation might have been qualified by a pillow over his face.

Duncan faced away.

Alan owned two little hotels: "McCluskie," he mumbled, beginning to encourage, "told me he had five guests last season with Jags or Bentleys who couldn't even sign the register."

Duncan stood with the immobility of a waxwork. The shadow of a cloud raced towards them.

"What?" Alan said plaintively—and loud as though a high wind had suddenly risen.

But it passed. And he added socially with scarcely a pause, as though this had been the sole topic:

"Well—I'll meet you at the Forfar Arms—at half-past three."

Duncan started to move away without a word.

As though confirmed, Alan murmured, "Okedoke—Lovely" —and drove in his spade anew.

But the morning had been wrecked. He could not say why . . . He had the most extraordinary feeling, and after a few minutes further digging he gave up with a restless four-letter, one-word protest.

If it hadn't been for the last summer Duncan might have had a hope.

7

J OHN LOOKED up from the bottom of twenty steps at "Duncan's mistress"—Ardriach.

He was surprised. Beautiful big houses are rare in Scotland and he had not expected the Mackeans to live in one of them.

He took this to be "beautiful" (even in his mind he gave the word humble inverted commas). It was the sort of house often so described. Surrounded by "a superb view." Proportionate, symmetrical Palladian. The stone grey with here and there little ochre and white rosettes of lichen . . .

From the fifteenth step he could not see another roof in any direction. Only miles of hill, loch and forest. Not even a boat. He thought space must have become important to them, almost like air to lungs.

From the great colonnaded porch, from a seat by a yew hedge worn grey as driftwood, from a sundial in a rose garden where snow had lingered, from stone, trees and country there emanated a sense of time past which he had met once already that day, distilled neat in Duncan's war room. Here, the raw material was more powerful. He resisted it, but the effort narrowed his eyes. And he said aloud contemptuously "Pah!" partly for his own squeamishness, and then on Duncan's behalf added "*Merde.*" For here the whispers of vanished years and deified dead must have played upon Duncan since birth—ghostly voices confirming his shape, his identity. The massive trees, level with those little— probably the nursery—windows, had probably given the highest —certainly the most flattering feeling—of which he was capable, endorsing him and falsely promising the same endorsement for his children. Perhaps the feeling had made his life, by grafting it to the lives of others, past and future, and to a place, a ritual and a role seem much larger than merely his life—and so deepened his identity almost to the level of a religion. The more elusive, the more religious, for not being really his.

Well there it lay: Duncan's intimation of immortality. John frowning went up, up, up.

A dog barked fiercely and then inhaled viciously, hungrily at the door base ahead.

John remembered stories of adolescent ducal heirs being sent here to be frozen, shamed and underfed into shape by Colin, only to be met—perhaps on these very steps—by Alan with a Lilo and a portable gramophone rasping "The Big Apple."

Like a child-limbed beggar on the front of a towering temple, he can have done the mystique within no good.

Alan opening the door thought John stared like a bloody tourist, stared in a manner that was a shade charlie. Limbo cottoned on and would have eaten him. "Aha, Harlers," he said, looking at his car and then with serious weariness, "Limbo—for Christ's sake pack it in." The dog, a coward at heart, gladly relaxed.

"Alan, what a lovely place."

People *were* getting charlier: it was that woman Nancy Mitford's doing.

"It's where we've always lived," he said with grumpy disparagement, "though somewhat improved."

When people like John Harling came to lunch, he wished they could have been here before—in the old days. Because what people forgot was that the sails of Puppa's legend had depended on a lot of suffering ballast, who never got a square meal or even any credit.

"Just walk right up." And then: "I hope you haven't come to talk business, Harling, because if you have there's a very nice hotel down the road."

John's smile diminished. They went in, to the rich smell. To the drink tray.

"I've got rather a start on you: I've had rather a bloody morning. Help yourself."

Tin came and touched John's hand with indifference—just in case he had an opinion of himself, like most of Alan's friends. "You never told Heinz," she said.

"I did," Alan muttered. "How's Robert, John?"

"I only met him that once, you know . . . with you."

"I heard he's sealed her off," Alan complained, suddenly reflective.

"Whom . . . ?"

"Jynx."

"But she can get out I suppose."

"Only by her own door."

Alan stared moodily and sniffed and sipped. Then he consoled himself with a gulp.

"He's got another now."

"Door?"

"Model. She doesn't mind."

Alan pursued his thoughts, already as though John had been there a month. But he was glad of a new attention, in which to publish them, from time to time. After a full minute he comforted himself: "These models are cold as fish in bed."

"Could we talk about my sister and your cousin a moment?" John said.

Alan's eyes drifted into focus. His face became heavy with resentment like a child's told to go and wash.

"I can't think of anything I want to talk about less."

He wished he had invited the Canadians to lunch and now perceived Tin's reason for having done so. *Pas de mouches* on Tin.

"Alan, are you happy about Duncan?"

"Am I *happy* . . ." He looked stunned, as though by a low lintel. "I've never been anything but miserable about Duncan—that's why I never see him." Alan's eyes went inwards like the claw-tips of a hermit crab in retreat.

"Duncan ought to emigrate," he said petulantly. "Canada's crying out for people. Duncan could be a firewatcher in one of those colossal forests. I've seen them. It's quite incredible: flying at five hundred feet on a clear day you can't see an end to the trees."

John said: "*Must* my sister live on a tree-platform with Duncan?"

There was a pause while Alan gave the matter serious thought.

"Well quite possibly," after which he could not bring himself to look at the long earnest face of John Harling. "The next step in Europe"—by John Harling. "Our Mackean commitment," by John Harling. Should he put the man in the picture . . . ? Tell him about last summer? if he blabbed Mummy would hear. She'd tell everyone. She couldn't forgive Duncan, really. Though she always kept up the "my own child" line.

"Alan—I think we *must* talk this over."

Silence.

"Just how well d'you *know* Duncan?" Alan said.

As expected John's attack fizzled out of his face.

"Hardly at all."

"How well d'you know your sister . . . ?"

John said: "Mary?" and then uncertainly: "Quite well I think . . . why?"

Alan was silent until he said uncertainly: "She's rather a sweetie."

He began biting the skin off one finger edge, pressing the edge hard against his teeth. He nibbled sensitively what the effort had yielded, and inspected the tiny crater with sudden total attention.

He said: "She's got Granny taped," but he wasn't thinking of that.

Tin, with grey receptivity in her hard eyes, said calmly: "You might as well tell him."

John began to look ill.

Alan inspected the fire. "Duncan's such a bloody fool," he said.

John said coldly, "Would you mind going on."

"Look, John," bleated Alan. "For God's sake don't tell anyone because honestly if Mummy . . ."

"I won't."

Alan ruminated. "Well, the Chief Constable here was with Puppa in the first war. Last summer he came to see me."

Alan bit his finger again.

Tin merely looked out of the window as though this was all his business, his family and now his conversation while lunch was spoiling.

Whereupon Alan turned to her and complained, "What . . . ?"

"I didn't say anything," she said. "Go on."

"Well, the old boy was in tears," Alan said with a trace of satisfaction. "He honestly was."

"Could you go on?" John said.

"It was just after Puppa's funeral. He suppressed a charge against Duncan. Now that's absolutely dead secret. Because honestly if Mummy . . ."

John said: "For speeding . . . ?"

Alan said incredulously: "What?" He perceived then that he was virtually talking to himself.

"My dear old John. There had just been a big poaching raid on the Cass. With cymag. Three thousand fish. It was just when Duncan's netting business was going bust. A river watcher got hurt."

"And you suggest . . . ?"

"The old boy said 'I'm doon this for Sir Colin.' It was just after Puppa's funeral. The King, Harling, was there. And a stand-in for Ike—the police sergeant at Port Alford was one of the pallbearers. He had been in the war with Puppa too . . ."

Alan swirled his drink, making a little whirlpool. "Now we can talk of happier matters," he said firmly.

John said: "No."

The eyes of Alan and Tin sank into impersonal solidarity. They waited.

Harling's turn.

It took time. The poor fellow was in labour.

"I mean," John said at last, "what one *must* know is: is it done with, finished; . . . in fact are . . . ?"

His eyes were glassy with consternation.

Alan went for more gin and said: "What?" from the tray.

"What do you mean 'what' . . . ?"

"I mean what do you mean. How do I know what Duncan's up to? Though I fancy not much. Paley asked me to talk to him. That was a condition."

"So you spoke to Duncan . . ." John was flabbergasted by the unconcern with which key factors were mentioned.

"I rang him up. I said 'Duncan, well stop poaching. This is your last chance.' "

Alan had never said so much about the whole thing—to anyone. Not even to Tin.

He went back, sat and began closing one eye, aiming at something in the fire. His mastiff moved. "Poor old Limbo," he said, rocking the creature with one foot, "did he say Eh em not my brudder's keeper? Eh rather think eh did."

"And was that the end?"

Tin said: "Alan!"—which made him say: "I think a little grub is indicated."

When they reached the dining-room he shifted the subject to boats which he fancied might be the only point of common ground.

John said: "But *now*. What's happening *now*? Mightn't he . . . ?"

"Quite easily," Alan said, on purpose suddenly, to aggravate John's condition.

"Well we must find out . . ."

"Then you're a better man than I am, Gunga Din."

John stared at him. Alan began eating. John said: "She *is* my sister. I mean apart . . ."

Alan knew from the tone that a scene was brewing, an acid scene in parliamentary language. His increasing irritability sprang from a desire to help John, or rather Mary. He wanted to help Mary. And he wished Duncan no harm. But God . . . His face became puce with resentment, for his own feelings. No one present knew what it cost him to say, "Well we had better make some inquiries. I'll have a wee confidential dance with maid Mary tonight." He began to put off the weight, to smile, "A wee hop, a snorgi. She's got rather a good sense of humour."

He looked up: would that do?

"Alan . . ." John said. "Putting it at its lowest estimate . . ."

"I'm afraid you must use easy words."

"What . . . ?" John retreated.

"Nothing."

"Is gaol for one's sister a joke?" John suddenly said humbly.

"It could be a scream."

John said: "I may only be a black-beetle . . ."

"A what?" Alan said, startled.

"A what?" Tin said.

"Let's be cool," John said.

"We are," said Tin.

"Yes . . . you are." John frowned bending his head low with closed eyes over his food which he hadn't touched. "Look. Are they in the clear now? I mean I know this education business . . . I see that will have to wait. But look—are they in the clear . . . I mean has either of them *said anything lately* . . . ?"

Duncan's back . . . half-turned as he stood on the butts looking out over the country where the cloud shadow raced . . . made Alan's eyes blink behind their thick lenses. He fretted with some minute reclamation of spilt salt.

"They're over twenty-one."

"I only want to know . . ." John used his wide eyes, insisting.

No one spoke.

Until Alan made his last effort. A speech.

He lifted his reluctant eyes—and the subject like a stone beneath which, as far as he was concerned, the past lay sunless, bleached, dank and slug-riddled. Duncan got an occasional raw

arse from Puppa as a child but on the whole special treatment.
Since he hadn't got a mother in the house Puppa made him a home
in the hills—all the more gladly because he, Alan, opted out at six.
He rather fancied Puppa had baptized him in stags' blood and
suckled him on a distant prospect of the paps of Jura. Duncan was
apt. He even wasn't a bad piper. And at fourteen he was stalking
by himself.

"I can remember being sent out with Duncan instead of with a
stalker when I was eighteen and he was fifteen," Alan said, but
was disappointed to see the significance of this wasted on Harling,
who really was charlier and townier than he had supposed, sitting
there as though at a service in Jap dialect. Even so, he continued,
when it came to the push at school etcetera Duncan always failed
to make any grade. He always annoyed *someone*. Who else had
been recommended for the M.C. *four* times without getting it?
Macky Armitage said he did plug quite a few jerries when most
infantrymen never even saw one except in a cage half-stunned by
25 pounder saturation. But it was no good—all the time this and
that little episode—disguised reluctantly by Mummy for the sake
of face, as wisdom teeth or the effects of parachuting. "One of my
earliest memories is of Duncan at the estate dance standing about
like Robert the Bruce, putting lairds at ease, and my father
secretly lapping it up, without ever looking anywhere near him."

The truth was no one really knew who Duncan's father was.
The dypso uncle in India was probably a fix. Duncan's origin,
Alan fancied, would remain a mystery. He hadn't really belonged
at Ardriach—so he had gone one homier than everyone. And
since the war he'd taken a turn for the worse generally . . . Alan
petered out at this point as though vaguely uncomfortable. He
raised his eyes interrogatively to John and complained, "Since the
war everyone's got a bloody great rock on their shoulder." The
complaint was in parentheses but nevertheless strong, and to his
mind more enjoyable than the subject. "I mean don't you think
so?"

But John, as might have been expected, was not going to enjoy himself. He said wearily, frivolously, "You mean Duncan gets the vapours if people put the milk in first?"

"What?" Alan said crustily.

After a moment John said differently: "You said his father was not your uncle. Who was he then?"

"I haven't a clue."

"Yet your mother had him here . . . ?"

"Mummy always knew what was good for her. Even Granny Lefevre couldn't have sorted Puppa. The only time she tried there was nothing left but the claws and the ovaries."

John's face became crimped with alienation.

Alan said, "The truth is Duncan's unemployable—except possibly as a tractor driver. But he won't do that: he's got such an inferiority complex."

"How many old Etonians drive tractors?" John said humbly.

"Dozens."

"All day? Year after year? For someone else?"

Alan didn't hear. He said:

"Mummy might get him back into the Palace. He was perfectly O.K. there. It's about the only time he was."

"The *Palace* . . ."

"He was Slipper Apparent or something at Holyrood. Chopper said he was first class."

John smiled wanly. "But, Alan," he said, "surely—it's what Duncan may do tomorrow that concerns us . . ."

Blood rose slowly to Alan's face. His eyes shone. Serious for the first time, his imposing heredity for an instant seemed possible.

He said: "Look. Two hundred years ago do you know what Duncan would have 'done tomorrow'? He would have rubbed me out. Like *that*." He made a slow precise pinching gesture.

It worked.

John sat like the stone deaf trying to cotton on. Then he gave up, keeping his eyes on his food. Sitting back.

Alan said: "Why don't you grill your sister?"

"Mary . . . I've talked to Mary."

After a pause Alan said differently: "I've often wondered how much she knows."

Tin said: "You can't change Duncan's idleness. He's a west coaster. They're all the same."

John was astonished out of his anxiety into an involuntary stare at his hostess. Even a class generalisation would have surprised him—but a *regional* one . . .

"And what are they like in Smyrna?" Alan said to her grumpily.

John looked from one to the other, then said: "But perhaps he could *be put in the way* . . ." he allowed a pause of liberal academic tact "of changing himself."

Alan plugged his fork through a bit of chop. Possibly Duncan might change you, he thought. The man was worse than Mummy.

John said: "I gather your father adored him?"

"He could do no wrong," Tin said with cold intensity.

"Except when he did anything," Alan said.

"Your father didn't mind the things he did," Tin insisted.

"You couldn't be wronger," Alan said with increased fatigue, "he minded just about as much as anyone can mind anything," and after a pause he added: " 'There are only two things that matter: In war, courage; in peace, justice.' "

"What's that?" John said blankly, examining his host, leaning right over and round so as to watch square.

"My father's last words to Duncan—just before he died."

John remained staring.

"You see you haven't really got a clue, have you?" Alan's voice lapsed to a penitent mumble, "I must admit Scott said he was faint by then."

"He saw Duncan last," Tin said.

"Which wouldn't have mattered if it hadn't been all somewhat Biblical"—Alan intervened to save Tin. "The kirk must have been quite a force in Puppa. I'm rather grateful to it—now. Because if it hadn't been for the kirk and Mummy he'd've cut me out. As it was he confined his feelings to this seeing Duncan last and entailing every possible stick on to my son or in the event of my not having one, on to Duncan, thus bridging the marsh either way, and ensuring the dynasty."

After a moment John said "I see" as though he really did, and as though the new information merely confirmed his attitude and the need for something to be done.

"My dear John, if you tried for forty bloody blue moons you couldn't see—except like a sort of aerial photograph taken through pink fog."

John's eyes widened slightly in ironic acceptance. He half envied anyone's capacity for mild day-to-day aggression, but he could not emulate it, nor, unless it came from an underprivileged quarter, such as Jews, homosexuals or Asia, could he approve it.

"All the same I do see," he said.

"I heartily doubt it. Pass Limbo this bone, would you."

John complied.

They ate in silence—and Alan felt, without risking visual confirmation, that John had resigned.

"Would you like to see Puppa's grave?" he said after a time.

People usually wanted to; like the Loch Slean dam, it was one of the things to see on the estate; and he was now proud of it. But John looked shocked and funereal.

Alan mumbled: "Nobody's going to make you."

"Well . . . I do think, you know, Alan, we should—I mean I must . . . I have so little time . . . I should like to *talk* to Duncan . . . "

Tin said: "Yes, I think you should try . . ."

After a moment, Alan belched with a kind of triste politeness.

In accompanying John to the door he failed to answer two or three remarks which John threw out like good commonplace gut stitches to knit the raw gash of the recent discussion. The weather, the date of the house, the personal history of the Austrian butler— were all apparently within the scope of John's concern, though he now seemed unable to look at his host easily.

"John," Alan suddenly mumbled. "You can tell Cousin Duncan that I've got twenty quid for him. I sold his boat."

They had stopped and were looking out now over the loch which was spotted with low islands like plates upside down, as in a Japanese landscape.

"A *boat* . . . ?"

"Yes—a boat, old boy, a dinghy to be precise. The *Achnasheen.* It wasn't actually his at all. But Puppa let him have it for so long, he probably feels it was."

This dispensation and flight of understanding cost Alan a frown which corrugated his forehead. "Though better say it was his," he mumbled. He dreaded Duncan's gratitude.

"*Good,*" John said. "I'll tell him . . . His old dinghy . . ."

"We all had boats," Alan said. "We each had a boat on the lock."

"On the loch?"

"As you wish. We went where we liked."

"*Good . . .*" John said, like a psychiatrist approving. He began to go down the many stone steps, sideways, since Alan stayed.

Their eyes met, lingered an instant and then Alan said: "Would you like to see what I got from Germany yesterday?"

John stopped.

Alan had taken out a little round red box. "Just step back," he said. "I don't want it to get wet."

John returned.

Cautiously, as though it contained a shy little animal, Alan unscrewed the box and very gingerly raised the lid.

There *was* something alive . . . something that pushed up into freedom, as Alan lifted the lid away, clear.

Slowly a miniature powdered rubber hand stood up with four perfectly articulated, dumpy fingers and a thumb. John stooped closer, intrigued. His face, so fraught with the conversation that lay behind and the afternoon that lay ahead, softened in bewilderment.

"A doll's trousseau . . ." he murmured. Then he realised.

And his expression did not disappoint.

Alan had succeeded almost too well—almost to the verge of

his own embarrassment.

"Oh . . . I see," John said. And then, "Do I laugh?"

"It's telling you to relax, old chap. It's just saying Tootle-oo. In a hundred years it'll all be the same."

End of Part One

SHE WAS just finishing the lodgers' room, scooping up the dirty stuff and the two cold hot-water bottles to take down with her, when she caught sight of a foot by the door. His big brogue.

"You're back," she said.

He had the immobility of a chess piece, with his little hands resting on the thick black belt which he wore like his uncle, over his kilt.

He said: "Well, did you ask?"

"What . . . ?"

"John."

"No."

"Are you going to?"

"No."

He let her pass. Not even looking at her. He seemed unsurprised. And although he had come up to ask just one question he asked it with indifference—drowsily almost—in the stiff formal tones which he must have used when showing the trophies to the Canadians.

From the passage she said: "I can't."

"You never told him then."

"That would have been the same as asking."

"And the same as getting."

She said nothing.

She heard him whistling a pipe-tune through a cleft tooth—a trick he had in mid-conversation. He did it with anyone—as though the farce of verbal intercourse need not be disguised as attentive and meaningful. Nor yet need silence be faced. Not real silence. Except when alone.

"He'll be coming after lunch. Ask him yourself."

He remained standing still. "Lunch is ready," she said.

"I've got to go somewhere."

"*Now . . . ?*"

"After."

The question which she would not ask he answered: "Business."

She stopped near him and looked at him. Few words had passed between them for days, yet her face was as involved as at the end of long dialogue. It is impossible to imagine what her thoughts can have been. Perhaps she herself could not have given any one of them a priority for speech. Fear, supplication, hope, anger, despair—and also desperation, all showed, subordinate to the unchanging inner dazed, hazy expression of her blue "childish" eyes.

Having not looked at him at all, in the room, not seen him at all in the house all morning, she now stood a few inches from him and stared at him as though counting his heartbeats by sight.

"What are you going to do?" she said.

He continued standing, still and incommunicable as a little stone god. She was offering, it now seemed, herself. Body and soul.

"Because you are going to do something. I know you are."

He moved, ceased to be the Duncan which Alan was at that moment discussing: "Well, just have a word with John when he comes, will you?"

It was his facetious chirpy, no-nonsense voice.

He went.

She stood with the dirty sheets in her arms and only when he was half-way downstairs she ran to the balustrade.

"*Duncan.*"

"What?"

"You've got to speak to me. You see . . . You've got to speak to me . . ."

The expression in her face, the infinitesimal jibbing of her head and her great, broody blue eyes as she made this hysterical announcement seemed to interest him. "Are you nuts? Because you look as if you were. Just cheer up. D'you hear? Cheer up."

"Then where are you going now?"

"I understood you to say lunch was ready."

PART TWO

8

EVERYWHERE THE snow was melting.

On the slopes of the hills dimples appeared as though knob-footed deer had been everywhere in the night. Water gurgled and tinkled unseen, till it broke surface in small, lively trickles, through etiolated moss and bilberry. The trickles joined the perennial watercourses. The burns charged down in jagged brown chaos which from afar looked white, thick and still.

The water drove through and between the ice structures like flames through the rafters of a gutted building. Gradually the structures crumbled, the fiery, brittle articulation, the clear form of icicles were extinguished: motionless one moment, the next they were taken by the general movement, instantly at its speed, the little snap which marked the event being utterly lost in the level roar.

Far inland, and along many tributaries, the hills slipped their month-old covering into one small river, the Cass, so that people who had lived by it all their lives and knew its habits, came and stared. The weather, they said, was due to atomic tests.

Deserted footbridges, of fishermen and shepherds, double planks suspended on iron hawsers remained motionless and fragile above pressures and pace which could have crushed them in-audibly in black jaws of granite.

Little ice now remained on the inner reaches, but near the sea, where the river spread and deepened in small lochs and marshes, and at the mouth—at Port Alford, whole floors of ice, which frost had thickened every day of December, were still intact. Here, between them, the flood assumed the swollen calm of satisfaction. Trees smashed as though by a barrage, floated black and sodden, showing no more of themselves than do seals and porpoise. The water was creamy, opaque as shaken medicine, and in spite of the expanse—a hundred yards from bank to bank—the phlegm (at first sight) of the current gradually revealed itself as a Gadarene headlong rush. Eddies and scrawls, flotsam and almost invisible ice blocks swept by as though to a lip, above one insatiable drop.

John called his sister's name through her house. Mrs. Barnes's voice from upstairs said low with complicity: "She's feeding the hens, Mr. Harling." The easy knowledge and use of his name underlined the complicity. And he heard the woman come to the banisters as though he might wish to confer.

He went out and rounding a corner surprised Mary putting down a bucket. He thought she had put it down so that he shouldn't see her managing its weight, and when he came close and looked down into it, this impression was confirmed.

"I love hens," she said.

"Rather archaic, isn't it?" he said. Her wellingtons were smeared and crusted with old swill. He did not look at her, because he was sure that what he had heard at lunch must show in his face.

And even when she showed no sign of suspicion his feeling of contraband information persisted and slowed up his speech. He wanted to tell her that he knew. He did not want her to guess.

He said: "I'm *very* glad I'm sleeping here and not at Ardriach."

"Did Alan read the paper all through lunch? I make him stop."

He looked away, scarcely hearing what she said.

She said: "What's the matter? Have you eaten something?"

"Mary—is Duncan within?" The Macbeth idiom was astringent —a help.

She said he had just gone. He was meant to be shooting with Alan.

"Now?" Each reference to Duncan cost an effort, a slight frown.

"I suppose not—yet. But he's gone from here." Then scanning his face she said dubiously referring back to where they left off, "D'you really want to see him. Perhaps there *is* no point . . ."

No point . . . his own words. He frowned. He was suggestible and enough people had already discouraged him from seeking an interview with Duncan. If she contributed then he might give in to an ever mounting inclination—to avoid Duncan.

But why had *she* switched? He could make nothing of her blue stare which deferred entirely to him.

He said: "Two hours ago you wanted me to . . ."

"I do still."

"Then what are we arguing about . . . ?"

It did not occur to him she might be "letting him off"—giving him freedom to have nothing to do with Duncan—or with her. And he did not notice her look of extraordinary timidity.

He became moody. He saw she had no confidence in "an inter-view." But then she did not know how much he knew.

She looked down the drive. "I should have found out where he was going, shouldn't I? I hope you *do* find him," she said impulsively. "Look everywhere. The pub first. And then at Andrew's. Mr. Deakin will tell you the way."

"Andrew's?"

"Duncan's friend."

". . . friend . . ." he echoed involuntarily.

"Andrew. Surely you've heard of Andrew. Colin's stalker. When Duncan goes away I go to Andrew for news. Duncan writes to Andrew. At least he used to . . ." Her head made one of its infinitestimal movements and she smiled openly disavowing any wish to tease or shock her brother which she was certainly doing.

"I see," he said as though he did.

At that moment Tin's Sunbeam appeared in the drive.

Mary smiled sympathetically at his face which was so grave. Seldom did his psychological stethoscope hang so clearly, so limply, from his eyes. "Mary . . ." he said. "I've got a thousand things I want to say . . ."

"Come back to tea."

". . . because what you say is most interesting."

He was looking suddenly rather ill, middle-aged and annihilated.

Tin got out. He said: "I'll try the hotel." And then to Tin he said: "*Bon travail.*"

By his car he stood for a while without getting in, staring down once more to the loch and the hotel, accustoming his eyes to the long focus, his nose to the strange fresh smells, as if for the first time.

In spite of all, even Mary seemed to want to make him feel officious. Or at any rate did so.

He was letting out the brake to go when she came from behind the car and knocked on the window.

"Do—*of course* . . . of course try," she said.

He looked blank and then clinically concerned because of her eagerness, her tone.

"To talk to Duncan, you mean . . . But Mary—I'm *going* to . . . now . . . we agreed . . ."

"Do anything you can . . ." she said. "Will you do anything? I really mean *anything*. Don't think I'm discouraging. I know you must think that: you're bound to. John—I do want you to find him. And have it all out. Will you try?"

"Have *what* out . . . ?"

"I do want what you want. But . . ." she stopped. There was silence and he frowned, slowly.

At last he said: "Mary, we shall all do what we can."

She laughed quickly. "Good." He wondered if he had not been given a toy to keep him happy, on another level than hers.

There was a pause while they looked at each other.

She said: "No I mean—you think I don't want you to find Duncan. You think I want to keep him . . . intact. That's not it." And then she added simply—"Find him—what else d'you think I want?"

He said quietly after considering her: "If I catch Duncan I'll make him give you a rest."

At this the whole serious expression of her face perished and she smiled, ballad-style, gay.

"I understand, Mary," he said, as he let out the clutch, "I do understand"—and when he was out of her sight he closed his eyes for a full suffering second. "*Merde,*" he muttered. "Send a goods-special of couches with squeaking casters, *north.*"

*   *   *

The new inn sign for the Mackean Arms weighed half a ton. It was a six by three foot, two-sided glass box containing six 100-watt bulbs, illuminating back and front the Arms of the Mackean family so that after dark a traveller would see the thing like a vision floating inexplicably high, far away, as soon as he came into that bit of straight. Alan had seen his lawyers about it, but nothing could be done.

Now it lay on the ground with workmen round it and Deakin standing a little way off—a slight, grey, relaxed figure, in slacks and pilot's leather flying blouse, watching.

In daylight, out of doors, the whiteness of his eyes made him look blind like a seer.

Duncan's car stopped at the pumps forty feet from the work. The white eyes slipped up and sideways fast, as when a chimp sees a peanut in a less likely quarter of the cage. Then they returned peacefully to invigilation.

Duncan blew the horn.

Deakin went up to the leader of the work party and spoke. Then he strolled to Duncan.

"Eight," Duncan said.

"Eight . . ." Deakin said, leaning in on the open window base, but not moving.

"I'm right out. I'm pushed."

"It's forty quid now, you know."

"For what we have received may the Lord make us truly thankful."

Deakin said: "Come again."

Duncan said: "Received."

The grey cheek turned slowly, fiery grey, like an electric heater coming on.

"So that's it."

"No—that's not it," Duncan said.

Deakin looked at him as though he were a sum—a complicated addition and subtraction.

"Urgent, is it?" he said. "Very urgent?"

"Could I have eight gallons, please."

A most unusual doubting gleam of incredulity came into Deakin's white eyes. He looked round the inside of the car, over khaki scarves, stray cartridges and dried mud stains; over Duncan's clothes. There was nothing he didn't seem to consider. Then he moved slowly to the pump.

When the petrol was in he came back to the window.

"That's just to make sure you get where you want, Mr. Mackean."

"Like you, Colonel."

Deakin's eyes, like little inspection plates of a slim calculating machine, showed swift activity. "Like me . . ." he said uncertainly and then they showed nothing—zero that turned swiftly into soft, destructive intensity. "Happy landings," he said, giving the car a push.

9

Habit. John made a face as he drove. The Mackeans were all as much creatures of habit as animals. Their paths were worn like grooves and their feet were lost in any other place. Even Mary seemed to respect it and slightly resent him as offensive to habit, disturbing to Duncan.

The road was navy blue with a white line like patrol trousers. In the village the TV aerials stuck out like exteriorised nerves and beneath them the temporary-looking cultures of frail council houses had windows against the gutters like eyes without lids; and thin, deformed doors, with oval Cyclops eyes.

There was a new tea-shack with a whole bunting of advertisements. Everything was bright, painted, prosperous. The eye got nothing but financially, for the moment, fair answers. It reminded him of Ardriach—or of a ventriloquist's dummy, a dapper dummy speaking politely on the knee of some invisible animator.

Normally he seldom drove through built-up areas without gratitude for not feeling literally ill—as he had in the thirties. Now Duncan or Mary or both had upset him. Nothing was right.

He passed the workmen at the hotel front without noticing what they were doing.

The reception desk was a formica slab with a visitors' book and chained pencil. A bell marked "Press" and smoked-glass guichet gave promise of human attention.

John peered round, wondering why Duncan ever came here. When he pressed the bell and nothing happened and nothing continued to happen, one corner of his mouth lifted as though for a bad taste. He leant on the bell for a longer period.

While waiting he stared round as though this was all a continuation of the conversation at lunch.

In a cartoon a fish said to another fish "The one that got away . . ."

In the sun parlour a young couple read two *Daily Express*es. The girl suddenly had her fancy struck by some paragraph, because with alacrity she leant near and whispered. This whisper, amid desertion, depressed John as did the man's numb reaction and the duplicate paper. John, too, admitted a dreadful inclination to whisper or shout. Life was going, going every minute. The purposelessness everywhere . . . People persuaded themselves they wanted specific things. If that were true, well and good. But in fact they just *wanted:* a verb intransitive, ever more neurotically intransitive.

Remembering suddenly his immediate mission he turned to repress the bell and in turning got a shock for, without a sound, the head and shoulders of a man had taken the place of the whole panel.

For a moment John forgot what he wanted; and then he spoke astringently as though the face before him had amounted to an invitation. Deakin's face always had that quality—even for strangers.

"*Good* afternoon—is a Mr. Mackean with you?"

Deakin paused before either replying or complying as though the words were a trap, the tone and accent an act. Then he simply shut the panel and reappeared, with scarcely perceptible sound or time-lag, at John's elbow. "This way please . . ." He opened a door marked Residents Only and said, "Mr. Mackean . . ."

A man was replacing a glass on top of the fireplace which was like a miniature cinema organ varnished with raspberry sundae. He looked up with bright bibulous eyes—a stare already loosened at its moorings. The smart woman with the *Queen* on her lap looked glassy but as though it were all lovely.

"Mackean here," the man said with a note of relief.

John said apologetically: "I'm afraid I want Mr. *Duncan* Mackean..." and he turned academically, courteously to Deakin.

The man with the drink said: "Sorry surr wrong number," but came nearer.

Interest showed in Deakin's face: "He's just gone down the road." Watching John he said: "Are you looking for him?"

Hadn't he just said he was? John returned Deakin's stare with dawning, bemused antipathy. What a face! The intimate *silky* stony kind of evil which you sometimes got in Latin cardinals and rural priests. The ultimate and absolute abuse of a form. In this case a cerebral form, John thought. And said: "Yes, I am," thinking of Duncan and this man.

Deakin smiled slightly, passed John and gathered two dirty glasses.

John began to withdraw. The American came a step closer. "We're from Ontario . . ." he said inquiringly.

"Harling—I come from London," John said.

Deakin went.

The Canadian's strong hand conveyed at once the unmistakable insistence of the Ancient Mariner—or a handcuff. Determined surmise in his face was met by apprehension in John's.

"Would you be kin of the Mackeans, Mr. Harling?"

"By marriage."

As though from now on they were brothers, and might meet annually, the man had John meet his wife. "Duncan Mackean looked in not long ago, didn't he, Amy? Ted," he called through a hatch, "bring a bottle of Scotch, a glass for Mr. Harling and one for yourself. Take a seat, Mr. Harling. Your best chance is waiting here. That guy's a chip off the old block . . . Why right now he's up a mountain probably."

Only a little strangeness was needed to dislocate John's drive in any direction. Today he had already had more than was necessary. Protesting, he found himself sitting saying, ". . . five minutes, if I may."

The man began to prowl while John exchanged courtesies with

his wife. The man seemed merely to turn up the volume of his thoughts so that, already in midstream, they became audible.

". . . I'm a guy that understands why people hike across the world to see Leo Tolstoy or Albert Schweitzer . . . they're looking for the person they'd've like to've been. Now it's Christmas . . ."

The wife moved: "Well, I think I'll leave you gentlemen . . ."

"This morning, Mr. Harling, I expected to see Colin Mackean again . . ."

"Yes, George . . ." his wife consoled.

He rolled a shoulder as though closing a door on her, frowned, shut his eyes and sipped. John saw fuddled, obsessed eyes on him, and felt inadequate. The Canadian seemed to pick on his silence as a provocation. Because his face became very determined.

"Never go back," he said. "Isn't that what they say? Mr. Harling, I'm going to tell you a story."

The man drew his chair close enough to be able to touch John. He talked. He kept breaking off to peer sideways to see where the bottle was as though it were in some way alive and reluctant to oblige. "Where's it now . . . ?" he muttered. It had to report every few minutes. Then his eye would try and close with John's and pin down where he had left off—hard enough and then harder still—what he wanted to communicate. He kept saying, "Colin Mackean" and then "No—no—no" as though John had been about to interrupt: that wasn't it? In silences the hand closed on John's arm trying to succeed by physical pressure where language was inadequate.

"Sir—'Sir' Colin——" then he made a face as for a mouthful of bad fish. "Tell you a story. Little runt—same height as Colin—a corp—never had a square meal. Old Kent Road. Never been in a kilt before. Now never out of one. Mackean tartan." The man sucked in his cheeks and looked sly sideways. "Trust him a yard or eleven inches say; if they were in front. And so damn' stoopid he'd walk straight into the arms of the M.P.s when the time came." He raised a finger. "Shooting matter in that war. A bullet—there. Colin Mackean used to go down the trench looking into people's

faces like a cook lifting lids. The day after this chap joined, Colin
looked at him. That man could say good morning to your guts.
Without a word."

Here the Canadian pursed his lips and widened his eyes
ominously at John . . . perhaps he thought he could finish the story
for himself. There he was wrong.

"Colin had shot a bloke who ratted—at a critical moment. We
all knew it. Now he stood looking at this little runt. Colin with
that bloody mace of his at his belt . . . Good morning . . .

"Next day—there was some shelling. Routine. This little chap
began to walk back to England. The M.P.s picked him up . . . he
told them he was taking a message from the C.O. to Brigade.
They took him to Colin. Colin said Yes, I gave him a message.
Did he hell. A few months later that little runt, when it came to a
scrap, was a second *Colin Mackean*."

John's eyes widened slightly in nausea.

The narrator stretched out his hand. All he could do was stare
and shake his head, as now the failure lay in John. "O.K.?" he said.
"O.K.? Colin Mackean," he belched and swallowed dyspeptically,
"and the mutiny—it was called a mutiny: the Boche stretcher
party and ours on Christmas Day—the knot—out there—I saw it
on Christmas Day. The cigarettes exchanged—lighting up—and
then a joker, we all knew him—putting his tin bowler on the
Boche—taking the prolonged coal-scuttle for his own. Two
orderlies went up. A fellow ran out of a trench with a bottle.
There in that place . . . stinking . . . corpses. A little flame—which
everyone recognised. A flame, Mr. Harling—as big as a—asbigs-
s'apetal—I remember the faces turned down the trench towards
Colin—waiting for the order. But he never gave it. He was court-
martialled. He killed close. With his hands. But in the same hands
a little flame that might have blazed into a miracle—*the* miracle.
MIRACLE?—Common bloody sense. But a miracle. Not history.
Why? *Habit*, Mr. Harling. He was *free*, only free man I ever knew.
No habit. Put on a tie in town? Yes. But you thought: 's got a tie
on. 'S got a tie on. Piece a material, doubled, hemmed and tied

neat. Urban human beings wear them in the west. Just because he put one on: I get an original thought. No habit. No crust. He was naked, nature . . .

"An' yet . . . Even the truce——" The Canadian raised one finger waggishly. "But I won't say it. Let someone else. For me, I'm here to see him. After forty years. Isn't that enough? Just to see him. And he isn't here. Where is he? Where's it now . . . that bottle. Hallo, Amy, still there."

He waved at her satirically. "For an ordinary guy," he said suddenly behind his hand, leaning forward, "there are worse things than war. Even that war."

"Most interesting." One of John's index fingers had crept the length of his face. "And you mean Colin Mackean affected a life-long reformation of the boy's character . . ."

"The boy . . . ?"

The Canadian looked up and took John in a bit, his position, dress and manner. "No—I don't mean anything—except what happened. Christ knows what happened to the boy . . . all the boys."

After considering John further the man suddenly raised his glass to him mutely as he had waved to his wife.

And indeed John's face had that quality of spectatorship which alienates drunks. He was thinking of the swarthy father with the mace saying good morning to the child's guts . . . *To Duncan.*

"*Most* interesting . . ." John said. The measure of his *arrière-pensée* prevented reasonable comment.

But it prompted him to stand up. "I really must go . . . I think it's frightfully important to remember the ambulances . . . the boots coming out first always struck me. I don't know why." He raised a hand diffidently towards his face in a gesture that perished and ended in supporting one cheek-bone while he frowned trying to communicate with this sizzled and dangerous nostalgia. "And the futility. Finally the futility."

The man smiled inanely and said to John's feet: "Boots . . . I remember . . ."

"Let's not compete," John said.

The man got up unsteadily, as though John were not there; he moved to the hatch but after two steps came back and put out his hand . . .

"Good-bye, Mr. Harling . . ."

*　*　*

John stood uncertainly by the cartoon of the fish talking to the other fish. He had, he realised, been dismissed.

He glanced at the couple still with their *Expresses*. The wife was dabbing her nose with her elbows tucked in, and her hands concealing the handkerchief. The Canadian woman passed with a self-conscious smile. A squall hit the sun-parlour and drizzled the view of the loch.

John tapped on the glass panel about the formica slab. It opened at once.

"Yes," Deakin said.

Could he telephone Mrs. Duncan Mackean?

For an instant it looked as if he couldn't. Then Deakin vanished.

He told Mary yes, he would go to Andrew what's-his-name. But would she tell him how to get there.

"Isn't Mr. Deakin there?"

Silence.

"I prefer not to ask him."

"Why . . ." She laughed uncertainly. Then there was silence. "O.K.," she said and told him.

"Then you're still only at the pub?"

"Yes . . ."

There was silence again. Why? Was she thinking his earlier determination and concern frivolous?

Now, suddenly, in this silence he wondered if all along Mary had really wanted him to "reason with Duncan" so nearly said, at the car window. He wondered if she were now speechless with disappointment.

"I'm going *now*," he said. "Mary, I'm going *now*."

10

THE COLLIE saw him first. It swept fast and low with barks that were shrill for his unfamiliarity. Then it fawned, despite his disregard.

Inside the cottage, Andrew Calder stood buttoning a policeman's uniform before a jagged sliver of mirror blunted with clay.

Above the open hearth a coloured motto said: "It's not life that matters but the courage with which you face it." This, a calendar, and a photograph of Colin Mackean in kilt and shirt were the only pictures.

"Don't I look a policeman of rockets . . ." he complained.

A woman who could have earned big money advertising tiaras or "Why not fly B.E.A. over the seas to Skye" stood behind him. She was poorly dressed. One of the last to be in black cotton stockings and without a middle-class overcoat.

She had been laughing and now she began again—showing bad teeth. Her black hair was bound so as to give it a "waist" above her nape. From there it splayed like a horse's tail to below her shoulder blades.

"Dinna laugh," he said gravely. "It's a policeman of rockets you're looking at."

"The back . . ." she said. "Louise, come here till you see your Dad."

A girl of fourteen came and looked from the door. She smiled —but only in deference to the general atmosphere.

"Eight poond a week," Andrew said to keep his spirits up.

"Ye'll deserve it for looking like that. Will you arrest me, Andrew?"

She began laughing again. A seductive laugh—from her whole body. The idea of her husband as a policeman took the very chair away from under life. Life sat down on its bum for her, here and now. Tears dribbled down her cheeks.

"The law," she said.

"Yer daft," he said sagely, doing the last button. "It's a special size."

"People would pay just to see the half of you."

"Which half? I'm a policeman of the Rocket Research, isn't that right?"

"Show Gran, won't you, Dad," the girl said sagely.

"Ach, she'll not understand. Let her be," said her mother sobering.

The old terrier barked outside in the sudden quick crescendo which meant a stranger.

"Who's that then?" she said. She went to the window. The light caught her against the smoke-darkened wall. Her bright dark eyes, cauterised by poverty, were still filmed with gaiety.

"It's Duncan, Andrew . . ." She spoke curiously, giving rein to surprise; even apprehension. She had not set eyes on Duncan since Andrew left the netting . . . Before that they saw him most days.

Andrew went out at once—"That's right, Duncan . . ." he said without *beginning* the words—merely carrying on with a sentence started long ago, years ago when Duncan was a child. And wrongly interrupted. Unnecessarily.

And in the same way Ellen said: "Where've you been? And we'd've sin you the night."

The snow had been neatly swept to clear the narrow path up to the gate. A few sprouts stood green for the first time in weeks. They were shabby, awry and dark against the white slush. Far below were two cars the size of ticks where the road scribbled thin along the loch's edge.

Duncan had walked with the uncertain, dilatory speed of a tramp. Yet within that gait he still strutted, and was rigidly straight. Now he stopped dead.

"What *on earth* . . . ?"

"We were just having a laugh," she said, almost beginning again. "It's the back. Isn't it . . . ?"

"Have you taken leave of your senses?" Duncan said.

"Let be," she said anxiously. Who was to know when he was joking. "We've got the light," she said. "Isn't that grand." She showed him, flicking the switch up and down. But left it up and then put dry sticks on the fire: in that dark room, fireworks for his arrival. "Where've ye been?"

"Well, what *is* this?" he said, still looking at the uniform.

The sticks crackled and fumed and light leapt up the walls. Shadows, as the people moved, towered, gestured enormously, became precise in a single limb, vanished and returned.

"Andrew was asking for you in the village, Duncan."

"But what's happening?" he said.

"Andrew's a policeman at the Rocket Research," she said, her voice hardening.

"Ai," Andrew said. "Eight pounds a week. And extras."

"A bloody flatfoot . . ."

"Flesh and blood like yourself, Duncan," she said keenly and looked at him. Why had he come, now, suddenly.

"My sister saw you at church."

"Did she."

They sat.

"Ah, Duncan," she blurted, "we're glad you gave up the netting."

Silence, while Duncan stared at Andrew.

Andrew, bent over his massive arms folded on the table, didn't seem to hear. She repeated the words again now almost singing them at Duncan: "We're glaad . . ."

"They were such crooks," he piped suddenly. "Andrew never understood what crooks they were. The whole fish business is an absolute racket."

Andrew was muscled as conspicuously as the prints of the old prizefighters which had lined the passage to Duncan's nursery at

Ardriach. He sat with his low shelving forehead and gnarled face like an old idol fallen and unable to speak.

"What . . ." Duncan barked at him.

"Ai it wull be," Andrew murmured.

Duncan's voice rose: "Nobody ever believes it . . ."

"Ai," said Andrew. "I expect it's bad."

"All this crap about stopping poaching . . . every hotelkeeper's a receiver. So are the big provision stores. And the Government know it."

She said: "Will it be just more obvious now?"

"Ai, and more of it," Andrew said. "More people doing it."

There was silence. Here Duncan had eaten and slept with his uncle; spent his last hours before going back to Eton, looking rather as he did now, and speaking as now saying they dressed in top-hats and thought they were God's favourites, and mucked around with cricket bats sometimes all day.

She could remember him—accusing.

"How're the bairns, Duncan? And you not telling me all this time."

He did not answer.

"And the hens, Duncan?"

"Shall I become a cop too?"

"Och away. Get you a big car like a gentleman and take me a ride."

"I'll become a flatfoot . . ."

"How're the bairns, Duncan, and herself?"

He didn't answer. Louise put tea and scones before them and her mother offered butter. "Fresh today," she said, and then after several silent moments she said: "Is it angels passing overhead?"

Each question that Duncan left unanswered increased the greater question: why suddenly was he here?

"Have we lost our tongues?" she said. "They used to come nearly off."

Suddenly Duncan looked at Andrew and said: "Alan wants to go after the geese tonight. Urgh?"

"There's a rare wind," Andrew approved.

"I suggested it."

"Before the dance then . . . ?" Andrew wondered, looking up.

"He doesn't give a damn."

"Sir Alan's great now, though," she protested. "I saw where it said he made a speech."

Duncan stayed staring at her husband and she thought so it was sport he was after. Like his uncle and the first day she saw him—twelve years old, soaked to the skin, sleeping there in the corner, while Sir Colin and Andrew skinned the beast. And ever since he had always come here for meat or when he was in trouble. Take the netting. A pang came to her as she looked at his face . . . like a mask.

"There's water enough in the Cass," Andrew said.

"And ice."

"Ai, ye'll need to watch the ice."

"That's what I told Alan."

"Ach, if yer careful . . ." Andrew said contemptuously. "Just slabbies and branches."

"Are ye shoor, Andrew?" she said.

Duncan was picking his teeth, his eyes absent.

"Urgh . . . ?" he suddenly barked, but so late Andrew merely said: "That's right."

"Trust Alan to break his neck if possible."

They didn't seem to hear.

"I'll tell him he'll probably drown, urgh?" Duncan said.

"Why will ye tell him that?" she said simply.

"It might make him keep his eyes open. Backwards."

"Ai, backwards," Andrew said. "Ye'll be watching the wrong way mostly. You should have done it this morning."

"It might make him watch backwards," Duncan said. "Wargh?"

He picked his teeth as though all afternoon he had been looking for a house to pick his teeth in, and at last found this one.

The aging stalker peered up at the sky. There was not long

before dark. And a storm was coming.

"Ye'll take a dram," he said.

"It's good you came to see us—and we'll see you tonight." She smiled—suddenly opening her eyes differently, giving herself to . . . a man, even to this one, with a movement, putting her hair back. She could not help it. The dance was on her beforehand. With any man. And a joking kiss with the uncle had been some-where in her, secretly, no joke. Nor in him. She had known that.

"The dance!" she laughed crazily, "I'm old."

The beaked face with collapsed womanish mouth turned and faced her for the first time. "Wurgh . . . ?"

She waited—slowly her smile died.

Fear touched her like one cold finger laid on skin. Because his eyes didn't recognise her. They had some other, absolutely private and engrossing point of focus, which they had come here to find . . . To be unable to hold.

"Duncan," she said quietly, as though waking a child.

But he had come merely to look through them; to find their voices dumb, the sky through the remembered windows different: people, objects without any kind of language for him other than the barest, literal, insufficient identity. All failing him.

His eyes dropped to her hands—and she drew them in slowly without knowing why, out of his sight.

11

"WHERE'S DUNCAN?" Tin said casually, and easily. They were setting out the paints and brushes.

Alone with Mary she always talked less carefully—and more; her able, dispassionate and anonymous face took on confidence till she looked like a Directress of People's Education in the wrong clothes. In this little house her full female body became not so much sexual as primitively political. She suggested a tribe where the women had won.

"Or don't we know," she said. And the defensive drawl of faint interest was replaced, now, by cool, smooth speech. "Mary dear?"

Lately she even seemed to enjoy the painting socially as well as financially.

"He went out," Mary said.

"Was that your brother on the telephone then?"

"Yes."

"I think he's awfully sweet," she finished setting out the stuff. Now she leant sideways towards a small table. "He's like you in some ways . . ." She was suddenly examining the Christmas cards which were cheap and small. One from Deakin was of men in doublets round a spinnet, and blazing hearth. "He's sweet but pi —and minds other people's business like you."

Mary said weakly: "How . . . ?"

"Why did you tell Alan's mother that Alan read thrillers in Church?"

"I didn't."

"As though anyone cared . . ."

"But I didn't."

"Oona said you did."

Silence was Tin's speciality. In it her body talked, with large cold physical superiority. But with Mary the point didn't need emphasis. So she proceeded—lightly, "Did Duncan . . . ?"

At last Mary said smiling: "Are you going to be unkind . . . ? I believe you are." Her head and body made several infinitesimal movements. But she laughed as though no personal remark had been made, by either of them, and looked straight, straight at Tin.

"So it was Duncan."

Tin went on: "I thought we might do this pattern. I cut out two roughs . . . one for you."

Mary thanked her, fingering it. It was kind.

"Yes, take it: Duncan is a silly little arse, isn't he?"

Mary just fingered the parchment.

Tin said pensively: "I must say I do rather adore that."

They started work. Mary said nothing.

"He *minds* . . ." Tin smiled as she prepared the stencil, "does he?"

The tone, with the faintest drawl, suggested the gentle dragging of a whip across a dog's face.

Mary said: "Perhaps just because he knows the minister knows —and minds. Would that make sense . . . I mean . . . or not?" The last words were rattled.

Her head went suddenly forward to say them and then, as though she had bumped her nose, she jibbed back, right back, until she was smiling, at Tin, smiling, smiling and agreeing to be weaker, if that would help.

"No. Some little Dickie bird must have told the minister," Tin said.

Mary laughed. "Not at all, he can see into Alan's pew when he's in the pulpit."

Tin dabbed her brush into paint as though deftly dispatching an insect. Her concentration in long pauses could have given the impression she had dropped the subject.

Mary's head was rolling terribly now. And her eyes shone. "It is odd, isn't it?" she said, "but in fact Duncan would never read a thriller in the Elders' pew. Any more than Colin would."

"*Colin!*"

The name had arrived in the room mysteriously like a third presence, as though Mary had involuntarily summoned the one arbitrator whose power and partiality she need never doubt; the man who "would never mention Tin"; a ghost who still, so often, presided in this room, in the village, yes even in Glasgow, and farther afield.

"Colin . . ." Tin repeated, beginning to smile . . . a broad welcome for the whole topic and the new arrival. "But you must be mad."

In church Duncan was outwardly like his uncle: he stood stockily, humble, and ritualistic—as though deferring to them—down there—and representing them, even acting via the minister as top mediator with the Other Level.

Mary laughed: "Isn't it odd. But Duncan doesn't like hurting the feelings of the people . . . *here*. Not here. Really." Then she added fearfully: "Not that Alan *means* to hurt people's feelings . . ."

Then she said desperately and sincerely: "Alan's awfully sweet. I love Alan. He's so funny. I mean, isn't he . . . I do love Alan. I do, Tin."

Tin said easily: "Yes—appearances are important. That's why Alan moved heaven and earth to keep Duncan out of gaol last summer."

The brush in Mary's hands continued to be correctly held.

"What d'you mean?" she laughed. "What . . . ?"

Her head rolled. Her smile became empty.

Odd words were then fed to her, doled out with intolerable cool slowness, and sympathy . . . a sort of detached theoretical sympathy, between the dabbings of Tin's careful brush. "I did really think you ought to know," she ended.

But Mary did not really seem to hear. Her smile became fixed. And the tremors of her body more frequent. She craned over the

little pattern, catered exactly for the requirements of the stencil.
She did not seem to know anything. Or think. Or feel. There was
just the mechanical painting.

After a time she said:

"In a small place people watch each other, say anything, don't
they, I mean?"

Then she added: "Perhaps . . . of course it's true."

She sat a little more hooped; her method with the brush a little
more emphatic.

At last she said: "Tell me more. I mean, if you want to. Because
you do want to, don't you?" And she smiled with her enormous,
blue irrelevant eyes fleetingly at Tin and then at the parchment.

"You know," Tin drawled, "Mary darling—you ought to be
your age."

For some time Mary did not answer. Then she said:

"My age. As it happens—I did know. I mean, I guessed . . . that
sort of thing. But I suppose being told—like that—is different,
worse. I know it shouldn't be, Tin . . . hm? Or not. I mean—
absolutely different. I suppose I hoped there was still time to stop
him before everyone knew. Appearances . . ."

And now she was looking at Tin—with tears rolling down her
perfectly still face, which slowly began to smile, as usual.

Then they worked on in silence until Tin said differently:
"Don't let's be miserable. Perhaps we ought to *do* something."

Mary said nothing.

Tin said, "Someone told me it was you who stopped him taking
the bank job."

"Did I? I didn't push . . . Is that what you mean?"

Mary's hands sank to her lap. Tin continuing to work, said:
"Would you like a glass of water?"

After a moment Mary said:

"He was so strange after the war . . . Something had to die. But
I thought if he stayed in the place where life last made sense, it
would be better. Or not? One kind of sense might be the best
starting point for another. I read in Dostoevsky that one good,

happy, childhood memory might do more in after-life for a person than years of moral instruction, might save them from losing their humanity . . . And it's true: because it's terrifying when you meet someone who hasn't got one such memory. I sometimes think John hasn't. He really hated (at one time) our parents. He wants to instruct people morally. He wants to order things; he does and he doesn't . . . And he's right, in a way. But 'losing humanity' . . . I thought it might happen quicker somewhere else. Indeed he goes away to lose it."

Tin said curiously and coldly: "I always gathered *you* had one of these fashionably unhappy childhoods . . ."

The reluctance with which she had pronounced the word "you" was matched now by the expression in Mary's face. "Me . . . ?" she said vaguely, as though the subject had taken a turn for the inexplicable. And yet if the remark had concerned her hat she might have become the topic with moderate enthusiasm and quite keen humorous vanity. As it was she appeared to be at a loss.

"No . . . oh no . . . no."

"We're both beginning to bark rather if you ask me," Tin said. "We'd better get on."

The post office at Croy is a cottage with one advertisement on metal and a red post-box let into the wall. Here the narrow road turns sharply and crosses the burn before separating at a sign-post which says "Cass Bridge 2, Port Alford 7."

John was unable to park anywhere near because the only available space—a shallow bank—was occupied by a large shabby Hudson, precariously tilted, with its bonnet thrusting against garden wire.

He felt that it might be Duncan's.

Rain in gusts obliterated vision through glass. Opening the window he craned his head to look uphill. The idea of living in such a place upset him; so too did the idea of having soon to communicate with someone who did—the owner of the cottage. Would signs be necessary?

Where was this Calder's cottage? Surely not that speck up there . . .

Although no other car might come by for a year he backed fifty yards to a gateway and then putting up his collar he made formally for the post office.

The door clinged as he went into the dark which smelt of sweets and cardboard and polish. There were begrimed brass scales on the counter. A chair squawk became an unhurried padding of slippers.

And then a middle-aged woman faced him, not as though ready for signs but as though she had always known him and he would be here perhaps for an hour. "Yes then," she said and pushed a single stray packet of soap a little to one side as though it prevented true dialogue. "Yes?"

He explained.

She came and stood in the porch in the rain, in her slippers without a blink and pointed—that was it—that's where he'd find him. "I told him he'll give me a new fence soon. And what's he wanting with a car like that when it's always just himself in it," she suddenly crowed. "No bigger than a penny whistle," she laughed. "And didn't he go and kill my Peter with it last year."

"I'm sorry . . ." John's concern would have honoured the death of a hero.

"Ach yes," she laughed, "flat as a rug. Well that's it then, that's it, up there," and as he retreated sideways, as though from royalty, she went back in, shutting him out.

The telephone wires howled; the burn he thought an avalanche of sewage. He took refuge in the lee of the Hudson and gradually, reluctantly took in the hell of his undertaking.

A gust struck the side of his face. If he was going he had better go.

He started out. The wind pierced his clothes. He pushed up his collar and sighted his footholds between the brim of his hat and his collar wings. As soon as the slope started he began to slip. His leather soles were incapable of gripping the slimy grass and mud of the path.

Twice he fell before treading carefully sideways into deeper moss and heather. Here at first he fared better though his trouser-legs were soon heavy and sodden cold against his skin.

On that day the whole hill was nearly, wherever it was not wholly, watercourse. Even in the heather he slipped often and soon his trouser-kneecaps and coat-front were chilling soft walls in which he felt he was knocking about naked.

After twenty minutes he looked up. The house was no nearer. He looked back: the cars were still close, enticingly close. He looked down at his legs. It was absurd. Alan had said as much. The sleet hissed through the heather, and he noted with surprise that although it was sleet, not snow, his clothes were hardening into crusts of ice.

Even Mary had tried to discourage him. Duncan was inaccessible—perhaps geographically; and almost certainly up there—should he find him—mentally. Up there—what could he say to him? Implore him for first aid probably. The irony of this joke at his own expense was not lightly come by: John's face was wizened as he admitted the ignoble fastidious limit of his resolution. But then he condemned as exaggerated his recent presentiments—about Mary's "state." Still looking up, and beginning to shiver and contract the skin and muscles of his back he thought anyhow —nothing can be done *quickly*. In a single talk—under arctic conditions. Nothing.

John went down and when he reached the bottom, numb, he took stock of his physical and sartorial condition. He had been right to turn back not a moment later than he did.

Inside the car he extended his long fingers. They were the colour of veins all over. He chafed them and as they thawed too quickly under the heater, he experienced acute physical pain. With eyes closed he waited for it to pass. He tried to relax, turning his consciousness inwards to the nerve endings where the exaggeration seemed to have its root.

When it was over he looked, out of his casket, as it were, at the remote house. And he thought: for the minute I have done everything possible within reasonable limits.

He turned the ignition key and was taking a last uneasy look upwards when he saw movement . . . like white boulders on the move. Sheep.

Then he saw a figure about two hundred yards from the cottage, moving from it. The sheep were converging in front, coalescing like flecks of foam, moving away.

The figure was going across the hill and slightly up it.

If it were Duncan leaving—he would not be going that way . . . where there was nothing but waste: a white, high lifeless waste.

Yet for some reason John's eyes attached themselves to the lonely figure with misgiving. He thought it was Duncan—without any possibility of ocular proof. Or was there a hint of smallness?

The unlikely course of a sleepwalker, crossing all the usual daily traces, performing in slow motion, as though memory were a burden as well as provocation, some apparently meaningless little rite of habit—all this perhaps had been unconsciously suggested by Duncan's manner earlier in the day, and tended now to identify that figure as Duncan.

A gust of sleet like a blow from a bunch of twigs made him wheel up the window. He sat still watching the course of that remote figure as though it contained more meaning than all the methodic point of his profession. He got from it a brown study such as can be got from a crane at work. It went on and on across the hill.

Suddenly an absurd impulse to shout possessed John so that he actually opened the car door. Then the futility came home to him and he realised with a twinge of fear to what extent he had been unreasonably engrossed.

He started the engine.

With difficulty he turned the car round the tilted Hudson. Then, facing homeward, he stopped again at the same place. And looked up.

He could taste rainwater from his cheeks, soft and tepid. His feelings, his reasons for being here lay about his head in pieces.

He thought: I might start back tonight—before the dance. Sleep in Carlisle.

The clouds were compelled in haphazard mass so low, wraith-like and similar they scarcely showed shape in the dirty white sky. Light was failing.

The little figure had disappeared.

12

THE WILD GEESE were restive in the big fields. Already below them in the town, lights shone—the brightest from the high window of Mrs. Lefevre's maid, who looked to the left of her long needle to see it at all.

Sometimes she stopped, peacefully, and closed her eyes. In order, a few seconds later, to go on.

Forfar House stands solid in reddish dung-coloured stone like an unmilitary pill-box. The worn road to it is bottom Port Alford priority; and in the garden the creepers, shrubs and weeds have overrun all pattern, like a green liquid boiled over.

The kitchen is lit with bow slits and there is a huge tower with enormous fish-scale tiles like an illustration in Hans Andersen.

Ivy makes a vertical grave of the porch. But of course it could all be changed, made gainful. The Royal Gold Hotel has let it be known that it will be interested, when the time comes.

Now a lamp-lighter prodded light, as pale as the first star, on either side of the door, and then slowly all along the precincts of the property.

And inside a telephone rang.

It stood—among dust-sheets but a door had been left open— allowing the alarm to expand in the well of the staircase and float up the great ascending square which was roofed with an immense opaque skylight.

The telephone chivvied with a long, sustained ring and then three peremptory short ones, but a grandfather clock continued twong . . . twong . . . twong—like the pulse of a heart losing interest in time.

The sounds had not the smallest echo, because the carpets were three, in some places four, deep, the tapestries doubled, doorways screened; and the hall windows, and wherever a draught-threat lurked, festooned with heavy velvet curtains.

A huge China bowl of ten-year-old potpourri was centrally dimpled like a marsh nest—for a clutch of four oldish gold balls.

Dragons, brass, archaic small arms and Florentine furniture, etchings of aristocrats and classic marbles all waited clean and presentable in the claret-coloured, discreet twilight. But waited for what? For this frantic chivying bell?

Such persistence must have sounded—if anyone heard it— dramatic, a claim made stridently again, again on that phlegmatic heart-beat of old time, upon the faint tang of unrenewed cigar, the silence of vanished children, the kept-up desertion.

Then—like a slow leaf, the last of summer's hordes falling, bent sideways with arthritis, yet hurrying as though her livelihood depended on it, the maid, a frail berry-faced woman, came down using the broad thick polished banister as a support for her whole forearm, and making no more sound with her feet than breathing.

"Yes . . . ?" she gasped. "Oh, dear me, but I don't know—I don't know . . ."

She caught her lip and laid a hand to her cheek gingerly and secretly, not wanting the person at the other end to see. *What'll I do?* she whispered.

"Yer Granny's taken a turn," and then suddenly flirtatiously and coyly: "She's ninety-*tew*—auld, like *me*."

Now she smiled, as though being proposed to. Then said: "But where've ye been then these five years . . . ?"

She took her weight on a chair top touching the fabric with ginger familiarity. And while she listened she turned towards the door that led to the stair as though to make sure it was only a door.

"Well . . ." she conceded, "I'll *see*—for *Goliath* . . ." and she giggled, young, like a tickled stage maid.

Mrs. Lefevre lay high in shawls and lace pillows, beneath a pyramid of tight grey curls. Her tired, strong, self-consuming face was smooth and pale as driftwood.

All around her the prominence of mementoes—lockets, photographs, everlasting flowers, bas-relief Madonnas, pressed leaves, pink-bound letters and drawers full of children's clothes—even above her bed a worm-eaten document of the first war—combined to make the room a mixture of Italian church and publicity office. Because the dead were holy—yet hers. They did what she wanted. They now, at last, had been what she wanted. And they were dead.

They had experienced the unbelievable, the unfaceable . . .

A long convention that the telephone was inaudible from her room prevented her from mentioning the snoring sound, far below—but she strayed from what she was saying—and only when the snoring stopped, resumed the perpetual litany, which face to face or on the trunk or local telephone she intoned to her grandchildren, and which, being lugubrious, nostalgic and apparently metaphysical contrasted disturbingly with her avid, practical momentous eyes, so dark the whites were blue.

But she did not look at the extension by her bed.

"Darlingest Kaka, Precious Lamb . . ." she murmured, spinning out a ration of energy for each word. "To see you there . . . my last wish . . . I see Alan sometimes. And Duncan. They're so near. But you came from afar."

Katherine, also, had a strong, tired, self-consuming face but with a low forehead and an almost simian jaw. Stubbornness and the ashes of wasted enthusiasm brooded, still hot, in her black eyes. She now wore a mask of deference—so obviously only a mask that the effect was childish. But it was accepted.

"I wanted to, Granny . . ."

"Of course, beloved."

The snoring came again.

They both heard it. And then it stopped. Mrs. Lefevre cleared her throat, youthfully.

"But he's been good to you?" she said with luminous pity, and almost burying the reply, continued: "Hm—Three. Taxed? Not taxed. A year—I know, beloved—but nothing now. Nothing," she whispered. Then louder: "Everything's so changed. Even fish . . . yesterday—— What? But still, three thousand . . ."

Her eyes for a mysterious instant were the eyes of a Pathan look-out. Then they hooded slowly; she closed them. "One must have faith. Alan is finding it difficult," she said.

Katherine said: "Are they going to go on living at Ardriach?"

The old woman listened for a stair creak.

"Augustine—'Tin' is it? She has quite a lot. They say she's *clever.* I wish I could help them. But everything here is Paul's. As you know, beloved. I gave them a little for the new drawing-room. Nothing. Some tapestry. From Varral. I had it still. I think he was pleased. He wrote me the dearest letter . . ." She looked sideways to the bed table. She started for it. Her hand moved on the shawl edge. "He said such dear things. 'Tin' . . . is it? She's *different.* What . . . ?" And in reply to herself Mrs. Lefevre muttered fast and hard, "Of course." Some *i*'s did not need dotting, and here now was what she had been waiting for, the identity of the phone-caller, so her eyes remained averted for the latter while the door sighed roughly on the thick carpet. Watford put her head round: "Mister Duncan . . ." she said, giving the name a slight arch emphasis, a difference from the other Duncans in the world, a place in the canon of grandchildren—but only just.

Katherine veiled, then dropped, her eyes.

Mrs. Lefevre moved a shawl at her neck, as though a draught had touched her. Great age was pointedly apparent in the faltering movement of the mottled hand and now too in the voice. She said: she was very old, she was ninety-two—"Send him my most precious love," she murmured, almost inaudibly praying the words: "I think of them all the time, all of you. I would have loved to have seen him . . ."

Katherine smoked, and tapped the ash discreetly—as though, if Mrs. Lefevre wished, she would not hear, would not see.

"Alas . . ." Mrs. Lefevre said and then, as the old maid moved, she added shortly, in younger tones: "Tell him Katherine is with me . . ."

The maid paused. Surprise was not left in her. But somehow she stayed. Mrs. Lefevre reproved the continued openness of the door by saying conclusively: "And my blessings to his dear chill-drenn."

Watford went.

"Yes," the old woman murmured reflectively and even now almost secretively, "Duncan's mother . . . you knew didn't you . . . some woman," her mouth clamped suddenly and her fingers contracted, then they relaxed, "she died bearing him. Just some woman. Oona behaved perfectly, *perfectly.* She made a home for the child. Colin was—*odd.* Not everyone thought him so perfect. Claude Lutyens—well I remember it—said he was really a primitive, *savage* . . ." She turned her head restlessly as though Colin Mackean eluded her, even now, dead. Perhaps more than ever.

Her head became still. She said, luminously staring: "*She behaved perfectly.*"

Far out over the estuary a long saffron rift in the lower clouds showed the winter day turning dowdy with evening.

Katherine stirred. The effort of obeisance, made easier by the ghosts of this house, still cost her dear; and now saying something she did not want to say, the words came out like a child's extra lesson when the sun is shining: "What does Duncan do now, Granny?"

After a moment Mrs. Lefevre said, "The days are so short. You'll be going to Ardriach this evening—the dance. Alan has done well they say since Colin died, hm? *Duncan's silly* . . ."

"Shouldn't he have taken the job Humphrey Harling offered?"

Silence fell slowly and deepened on them like snow. Their thoughts drifted apart while the failing light gradually wrought Katherine in black iron like a statue. The old woman's eyes closed. She murmured, "I don't know what goes on. He should have been left with that woman at birth. Where he came from. Colin said it was his duty—hm—to his brother. Highlanders are queer. *Primitive . . .* Little Mary keeps him." A moment later she said, "I want to be released."

Katherine raised her head and said simply, "Oh, Granny—now come off it."

"No, no. I want to go to them . . ." She opened her eyes, and weirdly they suddenly shone with seraphic certainty at the sky above the bay.

Katherine got up with a cop's smile and sat on the bed. Her face, now in a better light, showed a mask-like patina of make-up. Her latest H-line dress sat her more like a uniform, or a boast, than a garment; and her eyes were holes where sleeping pills had fed nightly.

"Granny . . ." she grated, her voice began to suit her face's absolute moral neutrality, her mulish tragic stare and her easily, quickly curling, farcically irreverent mouth which here and now said again, "Come off it"—but without quite enough confidence to carry it off. Only at the third attempt it came out quietly, curiously like a blessing. "Granny . . . come off it."

She took the old woman's wrist. She had been a nurse.

"No—I'm ready—I want to . . ."

"You've got a pulse like my new car."

There was silence.

"I couldn't see dearest Duncan . . . Ninety-four. Darling papa said he wanted the light over the bay to be the last light he ever saw. You were so wonderful with him . . . kissed him . . . when he was . . . when even the nurse . . . I hope I shall be spared some things . . ."

The telephone began to snore again. And again, and again. The extension by her bed looked remote. Another system altogether.

Katherine looked up at the door, and then at the old woman.

"This last month . . ." Mrs. Lefevre whispered and made an inconclusive movement with her free hand, closed her mouth tighter.

Then Katherine examined her at last with slow surmise.

Perhaps she had expected, like a clock striking, more of the litany, another avowal of readiness to "go." Instead there was this ... silence—and that untypical movement of the head and hand at the shawl's edge.

She stared and stared at her grandmother, and then—suddenly —felt the old hand press hers . . . *squee e it.*

Katherine stooped and kissed her.

After the kiss Mrs. Lefevre's free hand moved again at the edge of the shawl, while her large cleaving head remained sideways. And as though unlocked from life-imprisonment a little other voice came out of her: "It's . . . different. *Different.* Not what . . ." She couldn't finish but made a strange, convulsive movement like a woman in labour.

Then she lay still.

After some time she opened her eyes and said normally: "Precious—there's something for you by the light. The envelope. Nothing—nothing at all. Everything's Paul's. Otherwise . . . you know . . ."

Paper rustled: "Oh, Granny . . ."

Gulls which had drifted by the double windows all the time now took on dimensions of battleships in the deep black of silhouette and the confusion of perspective. The rift of saffron was rimmed with green, and the panes trembled, bass, with wind.

In a few minutes Katherine moved away. Mrs. Lefevre murmured: "Precious lamb . . . Good-bye."

"I should have come before, Granny . . ."

"I understood, precious child. Ah! If I could have had you longer."

The destruction of Katherine's face was terrible. It started with drops large and bright as gum, shining almost savagely in the long lashes of her cavernous used eyes; and then the strong mask cracked and if anything looked out of the crumbling kaleidoscope of cosmetics and efficient determination—it was an ageless, aged eight-year-old child, lost, fingering an envelope, and now soaking its clothes with pouring profuse tears.

The old woman closed her eyes and murmured: "There—go."

Watford was by the front door.

"Ai it's sad—but it comes to us all," Watford said embracing her, looking astigmatically at her ear to see her nose. "But you came . . . Miss Kaka, *Duchess* Kaka came. That was all her Granny wanted."

The eyes, despite smoky phlegm centres, were bright with prospect.

Finding her favourite unable to speak she said, to divert her in the old tones of coy vexation: "Tell Mister *Duncan*—that he's not to bring me down twice when I told him *quite plainly* . . ."

"What was it?"

"Just because Granny's ninety-*tew* people forget I'm eighty-*tew*. It's *fifty-one* risky stairs . . ."

The big clock whirred and struck. Four—solemnly, dispassionately. Perhaps the familiarity of that rich discreet timbre stayed Katherine's tongue with an overpowering memory of winter tea-times long ago.

"What did he want . . ." she said at last, morosely.

"Just nothing at all," Watford said. "A swittie. Perhaps a swittie from his Granny. Want, I said—*at last* Mister—Want doesn't Get."

13

THE STICKING-ON of a fluffy tasselled valance to the lampshade's bottom rim took Tin no time at all. Then it was finished. She twirled it carefully . . . "In six shades, moddom."

The object had the stark, tight, "gay" vulgarity of an unskilful tart. And now she held it high and still with a quiet ebullience which was not so much in spite of the scene with Mary as because of it. Today was good: fruitful in de-cobwebbing, ungothifying. It lacked only one thing.

She said: "Sir Alan Mackean, Bart., is going to be on the dot tonight."

"How clever of you." Mary sounded as if she wanted to mean it; but her voice was emptied of feeling.

Tin said: "I enjoy laying ghosts—particularly Colin's."

Mary's hands were backward, moving without verve. The drudgery of ugliness, of a lie, was worse than the drudgery of blank—like hen-food, ash, earth, National Milk.

She said: "You really think they *will* be back in time?"

"What d'you mean? . . . *they* . . ."

"Well . . . Alan and Duncan . . ."

Tin turned, an odd look on her face. Then she said with a slightly increased drawl: "*Duncan* and Alan . . . ?"

"Didn't you know?"

Thrust by chance into the position of being able to make a counter revelation to Tin, about *her* husband, Mary smiled blankly, unprovocatively to disown any suggestion of parallel—or of competition.

Tin turned away. She could not ask—so she stated. "Shooting."

"The geese—at Port Alford."

Tin's calm was elaborate. She smoothed her hair and felt it light above her collar. Her eyes went to the window, to the sky. Light was failing and the snow on the hill opposite was turning mauve.

"Alan is the bottom," she said objectively—and then added vaguely, "furthermore a fool. Can I telephone?"

When she returned she said simply: "He has left."

"I should have said before, shouldn't I? I'm so sorry, Tin," which might have been Tin's own words had she been in Mary's place. But the difference in tone was something Tin could not face without disgust . . .

She said nothing. She collected her things. The children burst in with Mrs. Barnes and wanted to see what Mary had made—and Aunt Tin—Aunt Tin they cried.

"See you later, little dears," she said, touching their heads. "Mary, you might come early with John—I'll need a hand, once there's a milling horde."

At the door she drawled: "Don't worry about what I told you. It all rather *came out* on the *spur*—— Besides: Forewarned is Forearmed."

All this was in the manner of a certain actress who developed a special style of Noel Coward heroine in the thirties. But it was provocative. Did she wish to "clear the air" all over again—because of her failure to "lay Colin's ghost"?

"Of course. In fact thank you . . ." Mary smiled—questionably.

Tin kissed Mary, lightly on the forehead. "I adore that frock," she said, half repentantly, trying at the last moment to squeeze out some balm, some feeling of some kind.

As she nosed by inches towards the main road a big car suddenly swept past, hooting heraldically . . . recognition and glad farewell. Alan . . .

Tin pressed on the horn and kept her hand clamped there. The insane braying went on till the Jaguar's array of taillights, like a distant fair, vanished. Then the Sunbeam's horn gave three mono-syllabic hoots—like curses.

Silence.

Instead of going on into the empty road the Sunbeam stayed still.

Mary watched it from the door, hugging her elbows against the sleet wind.

At last it moved—turning right-handed, home. And after a moment Mary went in.

John found her bathing the children—in a mess of towels, discarded clothes and wet apple.

"Well . . . ?" she said.

"Agh," he shivered. "Cold as brass monkeys . . ."

She sat so still. He saw it and paused.

At last he said: "I found his *car* . . ." and then he saw her look away, at the children. Her interest was finished, her expectation fulfilled.

"I found his car—and I was shown a house half-way up a mountain, *Mary* . . ." he protested, and touched a cheek into which only now was sensation returning. And looking down he parted his mackintosh to show the state of his lower garments. They were clotted, matted black—like a cow's backside.

"I meant to tell you . . ." she said, glancing down.

He stared at her intensely because she was to get this right:

"You haven't been on the hills today, Mary," he said. "You don't quite know what's happening. Without running spikes I doubt if I would have got to that cottage *whatever I'd done.* (He allowed a long pause. This was only the beginning but she was to get each stage right.) . . . These shoes *skated* . . . backwards. As things are at present. Anyhow—*in fact*—the shoes are probably neither here nor there. Even with them I might have gone up . . . if I hadn't seen a figure come out of the house and simply walk into the blizzard, into nowhere. A sort of dream activity."

"And it was Duncan."

"I'm afraid, Mary, I was not a parachutist."

"Stand up, darling."

"Mary, the point was: up there—on a day like this—I doubted the possibility of *communication* . . . even if I caught him. I did remember what you said, though. And . . . I do mean still to try . . ."

"What do you think?" he insisted. "I mean . . . up there . . ."

"Have a swim, Fiona."

He waited uneasily, for absolution, watching the bathwater swirl round the cocked knees, faces tilted with quiet glee as though to be in water were a secret superiority over those who weren't.

Wet as he was he sat and said benignly "Hallo" to the children.

"I don't know," she said, like someone who is pretending to have heard the question.

"Perhaps we were optimistic . . . ?"

"I wish you'd found him."

"Well, I mean, if it comes to that we can *make* time this evening . . ."

She did not reply. He could make nothing of her expression. At last and with difficulty he said: "Alan and Tin shot a most extraordinary line at lunch."

"About Duncan?"

He suddenly thought: she has been crying.

She said simply: "No one can bear Duncan."

"No," he said quickly, normally as though she had said it was raining when it wasn't. "Nonsense." He leant forward casually to play with a submarine. Many seconds passed before he repeated "No" and added: "You, the keeper you mentioned—me——: there's three straight away."

He shouldn't have counted hands; her silence confirmed the fear so sharply that he felt ashamed.

"What did Tin and Alan say . . ."

He performed a whole operation with a submarine against the duck. "Do they lie . . . ?" he said at last.

She did not answer.

"But *do* they? It's important."

"What are you saying, Mummy?"

At last she said: "Perhaps they do. I never thought."

"What are you *saying*," Fiona shrieked.

"I wonder what they told you?" Mary said suddenly, looking timidly up. In this instant she seemed to take some decision. Her head quivered slightly and she began to smile as though broaching a far more pleasant subject—as though at last breaking through to the Elysian fields of truth. "John," she said, "dear John, you feel frightfully responsible don't you? The Matchmaker. I ought to have told you much more this morning. What? That I slept with Duncan—among others—before you came back from Germany. In your bed. Mummy was in mine. We decided then. Before you came back. Am I being squalid—or perhaps . . . lying. Duncan . . ." Her head jibbed slightly, she continued to stare without any single feature definitely smiling and yet giving the overall impression of a smile. ". . . asked me in the dark how much money I'd get. 'Are you going to marry me then?' I said. I meant to tease him. I don't think he thought I was teasing. He really thought he was inquiring for my own good . . . He always wanted to be so different—a little king. Even morally. I suppose he felt he was informing himself about a possible subject's welfare. When he curled up—like a child, with those wounds like a great splash of brown paint on his back, and the one under his eye, his little, strange official face with its gash became loosened in sleep . . ."

After a time he said: "Mary . . . Oh God! So what?"

"MumMEE . . ." Fiona yelled.

She made an attempt at a laugh: "*Pas devant* . . . ?"

He said: "But all that apart . . . all that apart," he repeated with difficulty. "There is something else . . . I mean *today*. There is something, isn't there? Something else . . ."

"Isn't there always something?" Her eyes were glassy, he was now sure, with tears. "Out Ronald," she fished him out deftly. Usually she was as dilatory as the child—which now began to cry. She gave him his boat on his knee. The novelty appeased.

"But *today* . . ." he repeated.

For the first time she now seemed to be mentally engaged with what he had said. The first trace of thought passed on her face. "Today?" she said. "There's nothing new about today. Not really." Her head jibbed. ". . . No. There's nothing," she said at last. As usual the words had come out weakly, almost interrogatively and uncertainly. Yet perhaps a torturer might not have got her to take them back.

Two or three minutes passed. Then he said: "You see at lunch —Tin and Alan . . ."

"Told you Duncan was a criminal. Is that what you want to tell me? Could you fetch the nail scissors: they're by my bed."

He could not speak until he murmured: "Mary—why didn't you say, why . . . ? I don't understand."

She shook her head. Her hand, out for the scissors, returned to drying Ronald.

"You probably exaggerate; and you *accept*. And that's where I come in," he spoke louder—almost angrily. "*Poaching*—in Britain ranks almost with cricket. And if it doesn't anymore for most, it probably still did for Duncan."

"Even with cyanide powder and knuckle dusters . . . I do want the scissors," she passed her hand across her eyes as though a fly had settled there suddenly.

"I'm *so* sorry . . ." he exploded to his feet.

At the threshold of their room he stopped. Scissors . . . that was it.

"By the bed," she shouted.

He went in. He hurried in his search as though trespassing in a nudist colony, stealing glimpses of the big bed, of the long dirk with cairngorm knife, spoon, and fork inset, on the mantelpiece, and of Mary's old pictures in their art-school frames. Blurs— green wombs of country with visionary white deer forefront, lit apparently from within, like signs. He was dazed from the conversation, and moved uncertainly.

He found the little table and then the scissors too, but picking them up he caught sight of a scruffy commonplace-book, stained

with grease, frayed and dusty with face-powder. It was open—
with an edge tilted on a dirty saucer—at a poem.

He called out divertingly: "You write poetry . . ."

Both home-painting and home-poetry had produced excellent
results in several out-patient clinics: he had read as much recently
and thought it now, hopefully.

"I'm glad you think it's mine," she said.

"Isn't it?" he said, now feeling more license to read. And he
read:

> No, I have seen the mirage tremble, seen how thin
> The veil stretched over apparent time and space
> To make the habitable earth, the enclosed garden.
>
> I saw on a bare hillside an ash-tree stand
> And all its intricate branches suddenly
> Failed, as I ga. ed, to be a tree,
> And road and hillside failed to make a world.
> Hill, tree, sky, distance only seemed to be
> And I saw nothing I could give a name,
> Not any name known to the heart.

As he often pointed out—with slightly, only slightly dis-
ingenuous apology—he was "not very good at modern poetry."
Therefore after reading it twice and parsing it, he judged it something like a confession of visual schizophrenia.

But he felt that it reflected pain, had answered pain. Or was, at
least, a feeling. *Good,* that.

When he handed the scissors and sat down, his long earnest face
was more than ever solicitous, more than ever deferential to
Mary's life—things, happenings, motives, poetry which he knew
nothing about . . . But it was also dyspeptic with impotence.

She said: "I wonder could you read to them. I must iron
Duncan's ruffles—and my dress."

"His ruffles . . ." John said. And then: "Of course," almost passionately—realising a concrete possibility of assistance. "Read. Of course. Give me the book."

"I forgot—you're wet . . ."

"Give me the book."

"We've got to be there early. To help Tin."

She spoke as though telling him the rules of a new game.

"Good," he said. He respected rules.

He was moving away, feeling half sick with confused emotion —when he heard her say (she was folding something and did not even look as if she were talking):

"Like the others, you don't understand—do you: Duncan's not stupid."

She looked up at him: "I mean, that's why . . . Even if you had found him it might not have helped."

He stayed still listening in unaccountable fear.

She smiled like some women do when they wish to stop themselves crying and when they drive themselves to articulate what would be easier expressed in mere noise and tears: "That's why it's so difficult—why you mightn't have been able to do anything —without me."

"*Without you* . . . You mean to cope with his intelligence." He didn't wish to be sarcastic, but that was what she had suggested. "No, Mary," he said firmly, "I think now you're dreaming."

She listened to the word, how it cropped up again: "If I'm dreaming then judging from what you say I could have talked to Duncan. When a dreamer meets a dreamer walking on the hill . . ." She shook her head satirically and wearily for the whole conversation, and began to pick up the children's clothes. "We're going to be late."

14

WHAT WAS happening? What had gone wrong?

A few older couples in mid-floor looked at each other uncertainly; the band wondered if they were going down well. The proud portraits of the dead seemed to have more life, more confidence than the living.

Lady Mackean appeared at the door, went, appeared again.

Someone said to her, "He's in the bar."

"You mean the dining-room." She went and saw Calder from the door.

Beneath his broad shelving forehead, his little eyes, swimmy with beer, looked furtively round as though the trick, which had started at the funeral, were still being played on him; worse here than anywhere. Beside him the Canadian lent a drunken, willing ear. But the old keeper, off and on, stared round and, sometimes meeting a look like his own, paused and then turned away.

Tears stood in his eyes.

Tin said imperiously: "Andrew—did Mr. Duncan visit you this afternoon?"

"Ai . . ."

"Did he talk of going shooting with Sir Alan?"

"Ai . . ."

Tin browbeat him. But there was no contact of any kind.

"They'll be right enough, Lady Mackean."

The interrogation was futile. Bystanders, listening, merely gathered Lady Mackean was worried, whereas Calder thought they were at a pub. So her behaviour threw into relief what she half wished to hide—her "intolerable position." Only half wished.

She walked away efficiently—and after a moment Andrew and the Canadian continued to build an ever more incoherent retrospective affinity, clasping each other, and making a secret mutter. The First War . . . They could never quite refer to it—and yet somehow the omission was in everything, in every subject, above all in the man beneath whose portrait they stood.

Their silence was more expressive.

For when they were silent it was as though they had exchanged a key to each other's secret identity, used it—and walked into a single disused room and found there the neglected altars of a similar passionate memory. Then, with the impact of each other and alcohol, the memory stirred, incarnate, in the next word, which was always the name of Colin Mackean.

Nine-thirty. John stood near the drawing-room door watching reels. He was self-conscious, knowing neither dancers nor dances. To look too closely would have seemed critical so his eye roved, without any comment but benignity and seized every chance of a convivial recognition of anyone to whom he had been introduced.

He noted the kilts were a badge of commercial prosperity, except on a few patriarchs who defied classification and on the Early Man he had seen in the bar with the Canadian.

Suddenly Tin appeared beside him, to reconnoitre.

He had never seen a tenser calm. For the first hour she had moved with the purpose of a country matron who has taken in casualties from a train crash. No more beds, her eye seemed to say, but we shall manage.

Then she had said to Mary, who was dressed in white, in her wedding dress: "Will you ring up the Mackean Arms and see if they're boozing there."

John had heard the command: its cool presumption of total obedience.

Mary had said: "Yes, of course."

After that failure Tin's calm had taken on another dimension.

Instinctively people ceased to inquire after Alan. Only a jolly, bold, fat "character" quipped her whenever she was near: try the Fiery Cross; but not a water-diviner; and the search-party must be teetotallers, etc.

"Then you go, Mac," she said with strained affability and uneasy egality—and there was a roar from his companions: not him, don't send him.

John said: "Tin—can *I* do anything?" He had the impression she needn't worry: not at least from the point of view of appearance. A great many of the younger people, from the look of them, thought this was a Unionist Social or Northern Old Time Dances (Ltd.).

"They'll be here soon, Tin."

"They are vile," she said dreamily, as though praising one of the dancers.

Then John said: "Tin, I do want to thank you for being so extremely sweet to my sister. The painting's obviously an *excellent* thing . . ."

She seemed surprised past utterance. Then she said:

"We love your letting us have Mary so near."

This remark, which John, after a blank moment, interpreted as a quotation from perhaps an Edwardian memoir—or a just living dowager duchess, was delivered in the faintest drawl, as a dance ended. She added: "Just go to the dining-room, John, and see to the beer situation. Get Heinz if there's not enough."

When he returned, Tin, Katherine and Mary were together.

Katherine was different here. She wore jewellery which, being ugly, merely struck people as worth whole cars. The authority with which she approached, as though alone down a marble staircase, assorted here almost madly with the whippedness of her smile and the indifference of the dancers—and of her hostess. Yet, it is true, her manner, her deep jaw, lack of forehead and vibrant voice did, gradually, catch most people's attention. If only by sheer assertion.

"Wal—where are the male Mackeans? . . ." The tone amounted

to a taunt, also to a confession of boredom: she was only here to
see Alan. "Having a snifter with Granny." She made herself
laugh, and the others smile in different ways, except Tin.

Tin said to Mary: "Did Duncan say anything about going to
Granny."

Katherine said: "I saw Granny this afternoon. Five hundred
smackers. OK wasn't it? . . . What," she guffawed, "what . . . Paul
would have a fit."

Tin said slowly: "She gave you that . . ."

Katherine laughed now almost furtively as though on second
thoughts. Her eyes dropped, roved. "Just having me a little fun,"
she said, with the sudden limpness of lying.

John thought he should have gone back to London, as planned.

Katherine's eyes were now on Mary's dress. The white, the
youth. She began a come-back, her long mouth curling up, looking at Mary: "Duncan was never off the phone to Granny for ten
seconds . . . what? . . . But little Red Riding Hood got there first."
Now she was indeed amused, convulsed with laughter. Because of
John's face . . . mainly. Mary smiled at her curiously, as though she
knew that she, her dress, everything about her, had provoked
these words.

Katherine said: "Oh, look—John has swallowed his stoppings."

He had met her once. For a few minutes. She was laughing as
though ill.

"What did Duncan want," Tin stated. She could never bring
herself to question anyone, least of all Katherine.

"A sweetie," Katherine's laughter grew. The whipped curl of
her mouth increased at the very moment when she attacked most;
her eyes were infectious, they implored for God's sake a little
solidarity with you—and with *you* . . . the very people she attacked.

Several couples were now looking at her. Noticing, she said
louder: "Where's the laird—we want the laird, we want the
laird . . ."

"Shut up, Katherine," Tin murmured evenly.

"What! We're having a lot of fun, aren't we?"

Suddenly Mary said, smiling: "How are you, Katherine? How d'you do," as though she had just come in.

For Katherine had so far not said anything to her or even looked at her (except at her dress) although they had often met in the past.

Katherine now examined Mary gloomily as though she might buy her. "What!" she said with curt, defensive sobriety. Her face took on a cast as though she had been made to look at a photograph of a Belsen cartload: for that was how poverty affected her. "We've been around, haven't we?" she muttered suddenly in American—looking somewhere round Mary's stomach—and then, ". . . I've just had half an hour with one of your husband's admirers . . . a Canadian: he says" (and here brightening she looked at the others) ". . . Duncan's the split of Colin . . ."

John wondered if a slap . . . It was a sort of hysteria. Yet he had to guard himself against the fantastic assertion in her voice, her manner, that they were all in this, together. Everyone in that hall was in it together. Not just the house party.

"The split . . ." she guffawed. Then differently: "Andrew Calder made me feel as if Colin were in the next room. His beer got so watered down with tears I made him change it."

She looked puckishly round, for the effect.

Tin said: "Calder's a little soft, I always think."

"Oh no, they loved Colin,"—she took Tin's trick with a small uninterested trump; her first serious quiet words so far. She continued: "Duncan was with the Calders all the afternoon. They say he looked done in."

Her display of information stilled them.

"I'm Duncan's wife." Mary suddenly laughed. "I mean . . . did you know?"

"What? . . ." Then in a voice bored and puzzled almost to this side of utterance she said: "What's the game?" Then perking up: "Andrew's a policeman at the rocket place. His jacket's too tight. Why don't you ring up the pub at Port Alford. Colin often used to go there after doing the bay."

Mary said: "As a matter of fact we ought."

"Well do, then," Tin said.

When Mary came back she said: "Duncan had a drink there an hour ago."

"Alone!" Katherine crowed.

Silence.

John said surprisingly: "May I know—why that's funny?"

Katherine couldn't face him. She laughed to the others: "Well—he's obviously shot Alan."

Tin suddenly turned and went away.

"What?" Katherine said. "What . . . ?"

A new dance had started but the nearest couples were looking at them. John took Mary's arm and led her from Katherine, after Tin. His face was crimped: he could not bear to be thought fast trash; he could not bear being with fast trash; he could not bear what was happening. He did not like Tin's manner—but at least she made an effort to behave reasonably . . . "Tin," he said, "I'm most awfully sorry about this . . . I have my car . . ."

He offered to go to Port Alford, to the estuary, looking, as he made this offer, unlike anyone who would ever find a lonely country estuary. He was aware of this but could not help it.

She merely said: "No." One word he perceived to Duncan's wife's brother.

Katherine was trailing them now—with the haggard, accusing stare of a tart past her peak.

"MM?" she rasped. "What's the plan . . . ?"

John's mind leant on labels. Remembering she had been decorated for work on the Isle of Dogs in the blitz, he repented slightly. He said: "Katherine, I really don't think there's anything we can do—except . . . behave . . . as if nothing had happened."

She paid no attention for she was now looking at Mary in a different way: intuitively—and with all the weight of her own (and no one else's) experience.

"What do *you* think?" she blurted, staring at the radiant, angel face.

"Of course. The same as you. One has shot the other," her

head rolled, laughing at Katherine.

Katherine looked down with a sort of morbid uncertainty. The effort to sheathe her tongue resulted in a restless movement of her head like a dog with canker.

"We are standing here like a road accident right in everyone's way," John said. "Couldn't we . . ."

He felt the sudden cold of the door opening: Tin said: "Duncan!"—and John turned and saw Duncan in full Highland dress, dirk, velvet jacket and lace ruffles at his throat.

"Where's Alan?" he said. His voice was high and more than usually querulous.

Tin said: "What d'you mean . . . ?"

"I want to know what he got."

"What are you talking about? Alan is with you?"

There was a pause, then Duncan said: "Isn't he back yet? He must be."

"He was with you."

"Don't talk cock. He had his own car."

They were all staring at him. Tin in such a position as to seem to bar his way. The passing dancers looked curiously. Mary said: "Shut the door," and did it for him.

Then Tin, in the exact tones of a headmistress who wishes no washing aired before the other girls, said: "Duncan, will you come in here a moment," and she went to a door at the side—an old study, once the schoolroom. The others began to follow.

But Duncan merely stood. He said: "For Christ's sake . . . What is this?"

Tin said: "Come in here."

Duncan moved ceremoniously, his little hands supported on his sporran.

The room was cold and disused.

Row upon row of faded brown and gold theology and heroic couplets arrayed a thousand shelves.

Tin faced him: "Would you just tell us . . ." for some reason she could not finish the sentence.

Duncan said: "Alan?" as though they were all out of their heads. Then suddenly: "He wouldn't take the Jaguar down to the bay. He said it would get stuck. He left it in the village."

"But . . . weren't you together?"

"Only to begin with."

No one moved or said anything. They just watched his puffy face, with its garish crease of a scar, and his little buried eyes.

Duncan said: "He's in the bar. You haven't looked properly."

"What d'you mean?" Tin said doubtfully.

"In the dining-room."

They ringed him as though he might escape.

Suddenly Mary stepped up to him. She turned on Tin: "I simply don't understand . . ."—her eyes were brighter, bluer even than usual—". . . as though Alan wasn't out at a pub most of his life . . . all of you . . . your tone . . . standing there . . . always . . . as though . . ."

"Oh no—please," John murmured.

To his amazement she stamped her foot at him: "You're the worst of all."

Rich Katherine's morose eyes now seemed in tune. Her face, haggard with the pathos of one who is wholly compelled, now brooded as though given a moment's autonomy, a moment of numb relief by that scene. Here was no need for envy. She was even squeezing something out for them—was it possible—compassion. In those gleaming, abject rocks of eyes—there was a little incredible growth of sympathy. As there had been for death. It, at least, was real.

"He's not his cousin's keeper," she said—and then veering back to mockery: "Alan was lost for a fortnight in Soho after my coming-out dance. What . . . what? . . ." she passed the hat even now for a laugh.

But got none.

Tin drawled sing-song: "Katherine—I don't really know why you're here"—and she turned and walked out.

"We might get somewhere now," Katherine said. "His car

wasn't there when you left the marsh, Baby?"

She called Duncan "Baby."

Duncan said: "Christ! The Duchess."

She looked a bit defensive: "Where was his car when you left?"

"How do I know? He left it in Port Alford. We met at the Arms. It's less than half a mile."

"But you went to the Arms?" Mary said.

"Yes. But I didn't check every bloody car."

Katherine said: "Weren't you together on the mud?"

"Only about two miles apart. I simply don't understand . . ." Duncan suddenly echoed. "Alan's out at a pub most of his life . . ."

John said: "Of course. But it's late, Duncan. Tin's worried. Naturally . . ."

"He's over twenty-one . . ." Duncan said.

Katherine had got it: Alan *was* with Granny. Her eureka laugh also hinted his purpose there. "He heard what I got," she roared, in case they missed the point.

The tiny figure in eighteenth-century Highland dress, with his puffy beaked-woman's face stood with a neutral blank face. His eyes might have been holes in a curtain through which one could see white sky. Bereft of his two manners—facetious or functional, "official"—he stood stuck with the terrible lack of leverage of a fish on land.

Mary, suddenly, said to him: "*Talk.* Tell them . . ." and then couldn't go on.

Katherine said: "Ask the pub—if his car's there."

Mary remained staring at Duncan.

The door was pushed. Tin stood there looking at Duncan.

"Alan's car's still at the Forfar Arms. Locked."

A draught seemed to have come in with her—a draught of dream. John felt as though their identities were suddenly isolated from each other above a vast drop—which till now everything, everybody he had ever known had made into an unconscious assumption, a faith, like the floor of an aircraft.

Tin stared at Duncan: "Hadn't you better go back at least to where you left him . . . ?"

"Wargh?" he piped. The strange sound from his throat drew Mary closer to him. She said passionately:

"Why don't you talk—more?" Her face was imploring, wretched and insistent. She had no eyes but for Duncan. She alone was with him. But he did not look at her.

John said: "I think we should go to the spot."

"In a submarine you mean," Duncan said.

"I beg your pardon?" Tin said.

"It's high tide."

John felt impotence: he did not know about tides or Mackeans. He said: "I didn't necessarily mean to the bay."

"Then, Harling, you should practise precision."

Tin turned and went out.

Duncan said: "I've never seen such a flap over the as per usual," and he followed, with the stately loiter of a turkey cock.

Katherine was dreaming about it. Her eyes had sunk from being the least, to being the most engaged.

John said: "We'd better ring all the pubs in Port Alford?"

"Tin must be doing that. This telephone clicks when the other's being used."

Whoever he spoke to seemed to know, guess, feel more. And yet none seemed urgently concerned with *doing* something. John's face was wizened with responsibility.

"Mary—come through," he said: "You look cold."

Her outburst seemed to have shocked no one but herself—she went out. John followed her.

Katherine called after them: "Where are you going?"

"I don't know," John said.

"Where's Duncan gone to . . ." Mary murmured urgently and vaguely. She was crying. She moved on.

Reluctant to be such a sheep, Katherine gave a reason for following. "It's like a mortuary in here"—and she tailed on.

Mary led to a sitting-room full of stuffed birds. Golden eagles, divers, ptarmigan, black-cock and snow-bunting, all on the qui

vive in little glass cases of their habitat. There by one standard
lamp Tin sat telephoning.

Mary went near her and sat quite still. Katherine watched this
with an odd look.

John stood.

Yes, Alan had often disappeared before. Without a word to anyone. And loitered back: "I met a chap I knew in Doozle-dorf . . ."
could be his account of two vanished days.

And yet they listened to Tin devoutly, even to her long silences
while people at the other end of the wire went to look, to ask, to
make sure again . . .

The one light—behind Tin—threw her body into black bulk
and her face into shadow. Her voice had never been cooler in its
drawl: order would shortly be restored.

"*That's not what I asked* . . . I said did you hear anyone pass *before*
five . . ."

Then the exchange gave her an incoming call. They stirred and
looked at her—surely, yes it was all to dissolve, into nothing—
into Duncan's "as per usual."

Then Tin suddenly held out the receiver—let anyone take it.
"Mrs. Lefevre," she said dully.

Katherine spoke. She looked satirically delighted but her rough
voice took on an agreeable deference. "The harbour-master? No
. . . no . . . nothing yet, Granny . . . yes, we'll let you know. Good-
bye, Granny."

"She's got a nose like a trouffle hound." Katherine's laugh died
out as though in church.

A petronella had started. The jiggy music reached them
brightly and threw their still positions into relief.

Abandoned to practical inactivity, Katherine's stare became
almost suicidally morose. With no objects, no people to *affect*—
she died.

Mary suddenly said: "Tin, couldn't we go . . . ? Duncan and I?"
She sounded as if she had said: go anywhere, do anything . . . "I
mean why not. Duncan and I."

John frowned and pointed, precisely, in thin air downwards and said, with exquisite consideration: "Yes. But if I may ask—what *exactly* is being *done* . . . *here?*"

"The police are looking," Tin said, "and a keeper."

The petronella tempo increased and the scalping, wild hoots came now almost as though meant.

Tin raised her hands to her inexpressive face. She never indulged in gestures of this kind.

She was indeed, as Mrs. Lefevre said, but not as Mrs. Lefevre meant, "different," and this fact seemed suddenly to occur to her. For now suddenly as though she had only just noticed them she said quietly and intimately: "I wish you'd all leave me alone. And Mary—will you please remove Duncan?"

In the passage John squeezed Mary's arm and held it tight. "She's overwrought."

"Crikey!" Katherine said, half hoping this new turn would give her allies. She stood beside them. They were all in it—up to the neck.

"She's got it in for you, Mary," Katherine persisted.

Mary didn't seem to hear; or to have been at all changed by what had just happened.

"Poor Tin," she suddenly said impulsively and bitterly.

"I think *Duncan must* do something," John said. "In the car."

Mary said dully: "Where is he? Why isn't he here?"

"Come," John said. "We'll find him. Perhaps we had better go home. Perhaps we had . . ."

"What—*home?* So you're not going to Port Alford." Katherine seemed about to mock them, perhaps with a guffaw, for their new plan. John steered Mary past her, saying defensively: "There may be no point . . ."

Then suddenly he turned on her hotly. "It's not a game. It's not just 'fun,' Katherine—even if you think it is. Some people can still feel *something* . . . *without* a mirror."

"*A mirror!* What?" she laughed uneasily.

Beneath the portrait of Colin Mackean, an obsequious young man in a dinner-jacket was saying: "You could hardly breathe—six on each side. The French Cavalry bloke sat opposite . . . trim as a snake . . . twitching round his monocle . . . Sir Colin opened the window . . . the Frenchie shut it. Sir Colin opened the window . . . the Frenchie shut it. Then—you know what a train window's like . . . thick . . . well Sir Colin—with his whole forearm smashed the pane . . . one movement . . . and easy . . . and left them bare to the night. Bloke who told me saw it."

"Ai," said Andrew reluctantly.

The Canadian swayed and murmured.

Duncan was the fourth. He did not speak.

Mary and John came up.

Mary addressed him fearfully: "Duncan . . ."

The scarred cheek was turned towards them, making the near eye look too big, and inhuman, like something on the sea-floor.

"*Duncan* . . ."

It was like waking someone. Slowly her manner dawned on him as authority. He grunted a query.

But he came.

At the door a little man, a gnome, was talking. An actor. A local prophet. A buffoon. Which? His eyes swam with whisky, vision and release. He had an audience. And then he saw Duncan.

"*Hwell!*" he said. "Mister Duncan boy, d'you know I said today: I would not like to be *there* in nothing but ma garters; I'm asking myself who it is stands there, a little knob of a chentleman with his skirt all skittish in the hwind."

(Here he broke off to salute Mary which he did beaming and bowing in pointed silence. Twice he bowed, low, before her. Words he somehow suggested would have been inadequate.)

"Who else but maself or Sir Co-lun or the new Director of Edjakeyshun with his camera would bother with thon spate and ice, ai, ice . . . ice," his hand went out prophetically, "whole *rinks* enduring the dislocation of God, and going down to the sea in lumps. A great sight, to tell us ye are but as grass and tomorrow

are not; but the Director works, works, Sabbath and all, and Sir
Co-lun is gone from us—so who . . . while I shelter with ma wee
lam in the braken . . ." he pointed into the sleet fearfully—ending
fast, galled with curiosity: "Who's yon? Who *is* yon?"

Everyone looked at Duncan.

"And then," he whispered, "I said, it's his own . . . *Duncan* . . .
listening to the brown music of the mountains, watching the grey,
cold delegates to the sea . . . and quite right: where else—yes I said
Where else would he wish to be. It's grand to see a man that loves
his own."

"Then I humbly suggest, Willy, you invest in a new pair of
National spectacles."

Silence.

"Ach now . . ." said the small man blankly.

High and staccato Duncan spoke again:

"Your predecessor in that cottage shot his toe off in bed.
Because after ten years he thought it was a bat. When you pull the
trigger, Willy, be careful what you shoot off. There's one thing
you only get one of."

Duncan went.

One adolescent laugh suddenly brayed alone and then perished
from isolation.

"*Good* night," John said deferentially, healingly to the story-
teller, and half bowed in apology.

But without looking at John the gnome muttered something in
Gaelic at Duncan's back, and remained watching him, and then
Mary. At last, particularly, Mary, with stunned surmise.

15

"WHERE DID he go?" Mary had fetched her coat from Tin's bedroom and now stood beside her brother shivering and looking down on the moonlit ranks of parked cars.

John said: "I assumed he was fetching the Hudson."

She went out. Half-way down the steps she stopped and called, "Duncan . . . where are you?" and then on the gravel more insistently, "*Duncan . . .*"

John walked behind her as a benevolent old man might shadow a girl contemplating suicide on a river bridge. The insistence, the passion of her movements, seen in terms of the object of her desire, wrung his heart. He could not have been more excluded, or felt more involved.

She blundered a few more steps—a slow, untidy attempt to follow where there was nothing to guide; her shoulders were bowed against the cold; she was impervious to high-heeled stumbling. Suddenly silence and desertion seemed to stop her; the past years and months to culminate in one halted moment—face to face with the loch crinkled silver and lip-lapping in the moon.

John took her arm as though she were ill and led her to his own car. He wrapped a rug round her feet.

The front door shone above the tier of steps and the silhouette of a drunk moved slowly like a weed in a stream. A kind of X-ray by distance had happened to the music and only the bones—the drum-throb reached them here. They were down to the drum-throb.

"Is he coming?" she said.

"I'm sure—I'm sure," John said.

"We usually leave at dawn. It's quite early."

John straightened and looked at the sky as though it were to blame. The wind had dropped at last. And there was a hint of frost.

"The roads may be divine," he said in an ordinary voice.

The car crashed over the cattle grids and swept, without sound, over crevasse-like shadows of cedar and beech.

Through the windscreen heavy grey clouds, crossing the bright three-quarter moon, proved insubstantial, like grey veils.

Somewhere John had a life and work. An address. A little precarious language with just enough people speaking it to make it real; provided they kept together.

But here and now all affiliation felt tenuous. The small hours of this particular night had for some reason telescoped time so that he suddenly felt childhood and his own old age, and Mary's too, as all one moment. This feeling of impersonal pathos was one of the few feelings, of any kind, to which he had access. It found outlet now in slow driving and at last a movement of his hand in the dark till it touched her thigh.

The long process which he had been known to speak of as his "development" lay on him heavy and useless, like a table on a woken drunk.

This admission, however, merely drained his voice of drive. It didn't alter what he said. For to take the unsensational, relaxed view of any particular problem, and yet to avoid the grosser kinds of contemporary cant—this was his professional discipline and by now he was a mental-soldier of that kind.

"For instance," he said to Mary in the dark, "it could simply be that at this very moment Alan is merely pouring out his twenty-seventh pink gin—with . . ." (his flight of imagination induced a frown and he waved one hand) "some Coldstreamer or . . ." since this was Alan "some cashiered army dentist whom he knew at Shepheard's in Cairo . . ."

And then when she was silent he added: "I mean . . . do tell me . . . I get the impression it is not so much possible, as probable . . ."

He caught a glimpse of her profile against a patch of moonlight. Her head was leaning right back against the seat. She had slid her long back low so as to have all of it supported.

"Mary . . . ?" he said.

"I made a suggestion," he added at last, in a tired firm voice, ". . . you know all these people . . . and this place . . . I think, frankly, we should talk about it. And other things too. This may be our last chance."

The road turned sharply and moonlight slanted straight on to them. Her eyes were closed and her lips parted.

He had never thought of her as beautiful . . . All those tremulous jibbings of the head, those frayed fingers, the clothes, her sudden assumption and discarding of serious viewpoints as though they were hats, the general lack of integration, of personality, character, whatever you liked to call it: these were the things he had noticed. Now like a building floodlit for dollars, white as death, which traffic ads and jazzed-up, coloured-up sameness withdrew all day from notice, the moon showed her face, quiet and sad, in the peace of a transcendent reserve. Such a difference in kind from her life gave him a shock. He thought of her suddenly as beautiful, a word he had given up using.

She had got up at six, probably, and more or less run ever since. Twenty hours . . . including preparation of eighteenth-century regalia, lace—and the dance! And what else that he would never know . . . ? She was worn out. That was all.

Yet "Mary . . ." he said firmly, meaning to wake her, because no further opportunity might occur.

She said: "Alan's dead."

"Alan's dead." He repeated the words as a sort of nervous reflex. Then said formally: "Drowned." A feeling like weakness, like hunger spread in his body and loins.

"Yes . . . drowned."

"Cut off by the tide you mean."

"Mary," he insisted, "cut off . . ."

"What?" she said.

To be cool, objective almost cost him his temper: "Why are
you so sure? In a bay . . ." He began to drive slower. The descrip-
tion, by that old drunk, of the ice packs breaking up, now acted
like a hand laid on his arm.

"What?" he said. "Oh God, you mean the ice . . ."

She said: "It wouldn't have made any difference . . ."

John felt fear; an amplification of the fear that came to him
whenever he thought how nearly "touched" was Mary, his own
kin. For neither her remark nor the tone fitted in.

Then she said flatly: "Tin knew."

"*Tin,*" he said, legalising the tangent but asking for direction
from now on. "Tin . . ."

"And Willy . . ."

She was hysterical. "Mary," he said, more than ever firmly and
categorically. " 'Willy'—that drunk? Is he your informant? How?
That speech . . . A Highlander. A primitive. An *exalté*—who sees
fairies probably . . ."

"Willy," she said simply. "He's sweet. He played the pipes at
Colin's funeral. He used to be the schoolmaster."

John's chairman mind, already half sick with uncertainty, got
punctured even on the occasional concrete items which were so
desperately necessary for its confidence. He raised an index finger
in gentle protest and pause.

"Mary—you were suggesting—a moment ago Alan was
dead . . ."

He looked from the road, to her. She was sitting up now. He
said: "*How do you know he's dead*—From 'Willy'?"

He frequently looked at her but the moon was wrong now and
he couldn't see her face. Normally she was talkative. What was
this silence: was she crying, was she ill . . . ?

"How do you *know* . . ."

She said: "Duncan killed him."

What . . . what, he went on probing till he heard the tone of his
own voice like something separate. Then he began again. "I mean

I simply don't understand what you're saying. It's here, isn't it?"
he swerved angrily out to manage the angle, then turned, hauling
desperately at the wheel.

A sudden lack of deep surprise, a realisation that what she said
could be true made his expostulation seem mad as well as futile.

The headlights swept across the house front and the windows,
with curtains undrawn, gleamed at them in turn. She lives here, he
thought. She'll be here tomorrow. With him.

When he had switched off he turned to her.

"Duncan will be here in a minute," he said. Let her take it as
she chose.

She made no move to get out. She was now in a curious crouch-
ing position.

"Mary . . ." he said.

He put out his hand to her again. It was like touching a balanced
sack; only she heeled towards, and not away from him. And still in
that half-crouched position she put her face not into his arms but
behind him, between his shoulder and the seat. It was this sluggish
blundering thrust of her head which upset him more than anything. If she had put her face in the right place he would have felt
present, real. This moment was not intelligently practised for in
his life. And there was no feeling with which to improvise.

"*Mary*—what is it? I am *here*. There. I think first of all that you
are terribly overtired. I shall say to my mother that you must go
home for a month at least. Or my mother can bloody well come
here."

She began to sob, trembling convulsively. He could remember
in childhood tears that poured from an undisturbed, even a
smiling face. But never a sound, never this.

With the impersonality of a ventriloquist he managed to allude
to her statement. "Can't you say more? . . . I mean aren't you
imagining?"

He stared at her bowed shoulders, below him in the dark.

"The old man you mean . . . seeing Duncan. Was that it?"

He himself now saw, imagined, the destination of Duncan's

strange route across the hills, saw Duncan like a monstrous little chess-piece stock-still, impervious to numbing sleet above the mouth of the Cass River. On some vantage point . . . *an eminence.*

John looked away—up and round at the garden as though for relief. Then his eyes stayed still: something had moved.

A tree sprouted a faint shadow like white smoke. It veered and vanished.

Suddenly she cried out quietly: "Oh what is there . . . what is there . . ."

The tree's shadow came strong and swept now in the other direction. Some dead pampas stalks turned to a sheaf of silver wire and then again there was darkness.

Her head moved.

"I can stay till tomorrow," he said. "We had better go in now."

"I can stay," he repeated.

"No."

She sat up and said almost normally: "We must go in." Then she rummaged in her bag.

He got out. Going into the house he held her tightly above the arm as though she were an old woman and might slip. He walked stiffly and slightly awry.

He said: "Alan may be perfectly all right."

Reasonably, she said: "Yes."

It was the lights and the usual objects in the hall which made his suggestion, and its tone, possible. They were waking up. In the car she had dreamt. Why, of course, he suddenly thought, her eyes *were* closed. And he was able to suddenly boom an ironic "Aggh!" like someone coming out of a bad film.

"Of course he is," he added, gathering way. "What time did you get up this morning?"

"Time!"

"Seriously."

"Fiona called at five."

He made a gesture—almost impatient, irritated. He had been lured into an untidy, embarrassing, unnecessary scene. A fantastic

—a perfectly *fantastic* orgy of . . . "Aft," he said aloud and then:
"Mary—it's true I ought to be going in the morning."

"Of course. You must go."

"This evening was most regrettable. But I gather Tin is inured
to it."

She almost managed astonishment as she looked up at him.
They were still in the passage. But he continued to summarise and
regulate.

"Even so, Mary, we will keep in touch . . ." he was frowning at
her as though she had done something wrong, "and as soon as I get
back, you will come and stay with me in London. For a rest. Our
mother will take the children? . . . She can't maim them in a
month."

At the door of the living-room Mary put on the wan four
pointed bulbs of the miniature chandelier. It showed the remains
of the children's supper, and an old bedroom hot-water can with
which she had been topping-up the heaters for the morning, when
they had to leave for the evening.

"Would you like something . . . ?" she said.

Her back, the shape of it, was not right. He suddenly said
irritably: "Because, Mary—it simply didn't happen . . . as you
supposed."

"What time do you start?" She made it clear he had not spoken.
But a smile—that is to say a merely normal look from her eyes—
for a fleeting second had the effect of galling him still further. His
face was crabbed.

"Well, nine. But we can see . . ." He was frowning at her neck
thinking she probably doesn't give herself proper food.

Duncan's headlights flashed at the gate and the tyre sounded on
the gravel.

Their eyes met—but through the bars of her perpetual smile,
which now, less than ever before, could he trace to one feature.

Dropping his voice to a low murmur he said intensely: "You
know what you said: '*killed.*' Good: it was a *façon de parler*. If an
accident *has* happened then you were suggesting carelessness—

criminal carelessness, i.e.: Duncan didn't *do* anything . . ."

For a moment her reluctance to reply confirmed hope and then slowly killed it.

"What?" he said.

"D'you want to go on? No—he didn't do anything. He didn't have to."

"How can you *know?*" he cajoled, implored.

"He knew the bay so well—he only had to wish: the rest was done for him. By the bay."

For several seconds he was silent.

"Mary—supposing what you say were true. Good heavens. This is morbid. Habit is a great protection. If wishing were a crime —how many murderers there would be."

The remark cost him something. It felt like someone else's. She said: "Must we?" Then: "I wonder. Wouldn't many abandon the wish if the opportunity to realise that wish—were secretly offered? Surely most. Even now."

Now she was using his "position." Confusion destroyed him.

"Anyhow, what do you mean 'Even now' . . . ?" he said with hostility. "In what sense are you generalising?"

She said: "You think it's just Duncan—or just the Mackeans— or people like them. But isn't there a kind of vacuum in people's hearts—into which . . . anything can walk? While outwardly . . ."

"The vacuum *could* of course be in you."

"Oh yes it could, it could. It *is*. Why are we talking like this . . ." she said miserably, ". . . as though nothing has really happened? You love theory."

"It can help to stand at a distance . . ."

"You mean verbally at a million miles . . ." she said.

Duncan's steps were audible. They were left staring at each other. John closed his eyes a moment.

"I think I'll go up. Mary . . . it would be unreasonable to suppose that I could be of . . .——" he finished with his eyes.

"Of course. Good night, John."

"Why don't you come up . . . ?"

"I must lay breakfast, and do the fires."

"I see . . ." He lingered.

"No *please*—go up."

At the top of the stairs he stopped.

He looked back down, deprived of will-power. The impulse was too feeble and died when Duncan loitered by, stately and erect, going into the living-room.

The door slammed.

In his room he sat down on the edge of the bed. A gloom like a tight illness had risen inside him. He could muster no energy to move or do anything. A print of a carriage in the Place Vendôme bound in passe-partout, a wedding present probably, and a gay coloured china Scots piper, suddenly struck him, innocent objects though they were, as mad, criminal, impossible.

How long did he stay thus?

It was later. He was lying back still dressed. He heard a movement and there she was at the door.

"I've got to talk—d'you mind? You'll be gone soon—I've got —I'm so sorry this has happened, John, on your first visit. I mean I am—really . . ."

She sat down on the end of the bed and her head jibbed a little as she met his eyes.

"My dear Mary—*think* . . . And then don't talk like that anymore . . ."

"Then forget what I said. Will you . . . ? Please—you must forget it. I want you to promise—now—here. Will you . . . ?"

"Of course—I have already forgotten . . ." And indeed as he looked into her stupefied eyes he thought how could he ever have taken what she said as meaning anything but exhaustion and hysteria: "Mary—one thing I do counsel you: go to bed *now*— and take something really hefty to make you sleep. Don't you think?"

And then to his surprise she turned her head from him stickily, sluggishly like soldiers leaving cover that has proved worse than the open.

His sense of inadequacy increased. "What can I say, Mary? Or do? Tell me . . . Nothing is certain. Is it—yet. Even that there's been an accident . . ."

After a moment's silence he said: "But do—tell me about Duncan. And everything. Of course—how could I for a moment suppose what you suggested—in your sleep—was true. But I do submit to you—that this life, which you lead here, is *incestuous* . . ." He here studied her face hopefully and compellingly. "He is in love with things he should have left—long ago. Soil, place, family, the past—roots. And you, Mary—don't you perhaps take pleasure in protecting him in perpetuating this illusory security? One must have the courage to travel light today."

She looked at him oddly as though for a second interest in him as a specimen cut through the predicament—and even yes—as she looked longer endowed him with a mad relevance.

Dreamily, stupidly, she said: "You and Duncan are the same person," and then she timidly turned away as though to hide her face from his concerned, sensible reaction of absolute vacance.

She said: "I spoke to Duncan just now. I asked a question . . ." She was silent and her body trembled. "He didn't hear . . . he didn't hear . . . Or rather he didn't 'for a minute suppose that what I suggested was true.' "

To hear his words quoted back at him in this context affected John unpleasantly. As he fell silent his eyes warned her: he had not *wished* to say *anything*.

In a jerky monotone she said: "Duncan was weak—how weak and if you like . . . 'insignificant.' " (Whom and how many he suddenly wondered was she quoting?) "So we made as you foresaw a good match."

"You supported his identity," he suddenly interrupted aggressively, feeling suddenly she, more than he had ever suspected, could look after herself.

For some time she could not manage the switch. Her face

clouded with the effort. She had to *feel* each subject, divine it.

"You talk of identity as though it were a hat. To put on and off. You don't know what is dying in the world. You think a hat is dying. If your capacity for identity is a hat—then . . ."

She shook her head, closing her eyes.

He said: "You were telling me about Duncan."

So long was her silence he contemplated moving her to her room and had even got up to do so when she said:

"It was a Sunday in winter two years ago. Jean had a cold. It was sunny. She was in the porch. He came in and I said: 'Some men came and took the lorry.' Six of them had taken it openly without a word, even when I asked them, to their faces. He said: 'I sold it to them.' I said: 'That isn't true.' He shouted at me . . . He turned round and I said 'Duncan' looking at him. That is the point: he wasn't there: he didn't hear or see me."

She began to cry quietly and then at last laughed in the middle and stopped. "He had lost his hat," she suddenly said statistically. "He lost his hat on the ice."

Her face became settled, abstract, her eyes without focus. She said: "A shadow—no bigger than a feeling of nothing. Then the sleepwalk starts."

She looked up slowly, stubbornly, and their eyes met: a step had sounded on the foot of the stairs. For a few seconds the silence was qualified, made ordinary by a pipe-tune, whistled through the front teeth. Then that too stopped.

There was absolute silence while they continued to stare into each other's faces. Then she smiled. Slowly and remotely, how remotely as though she existed where nothing reached.

He knew then that they would not meet again, perhaps for years, certainly not the next morning. And he knew they had never met before—and that what she had said in the car was true; and that she had known it was possible when she greeted him, smiling, in the morning.

The dawn broke over the bay at first with the faint sheen of a fish belly below surface; then it spread higher, paler till the confusion of lights was made clear on different, solid levels. The radar mast-head became separate from the hills, and the town from its reflection in the water.

A stertorous, always penultimate puffing gave place to a violent clatter from the siding. The air became full of the noise of wings, and the water-logged tree, like an overturned hieroglyph, had a deep rushing wake as though it sped inland.

Today its outline was altered: different branches showed against the sky. A great slab of ice, half tilted by the pressure of the current, was pushing a huge shoddy beak into the sodden trunk. Water poured over its shoulders splashing and roaring either side.

In one turbulent gap, circumscribed by the ice, the trunk and a lateral branch, a curved bulk like someone praying, seen from above, moved slightly back and forth in the constancy of an obscure impulse. Wet cloth stayed ballooned with air and some skin showed pale as cheese rind. But what skin, skin of what part? Such a gleam, in such shapelessness, would soon violate the eyes, the heart's capacity to accept—until clumsy movements turned up a face, blinded, inert, killed—a definition of proof before which reason would vanish in the surge of a more immediate and deeper appreciation.

Now light showed the sea and the unplaceable limit between it and the sky, and on the shore a knot of men, coming through the spiny grass toward the mud, pointing, searching and calling to each other.

DALKEY ARCHIVE PAPERBACKS

FICTION

BARNES, DJUNA. *Ryder*	9.95
CRAWFORD, STANLEY. *Some Instructions to My Wife*	7.95
CUSACK, RALPH. *Cadenza*	7.95
DOWELL, COLEMAN. *Too Much Flesh and Jabez*	8.00
ERNAUX, ANNIE. *Cleaned Out*	9.95
FIRBANK, RONALD. *Complete Short Stories*	9.95
GASS, WILLIAM H. *Willie Masters' Lonesome Wife*	7.95
GRAINVILLE, PATRICK. *The Cave of Heaven*	9.95
MacLOCHLAINN, ALF. *Out of Focus*	5.95
MARKSON, DAVID. *Springer's Progress*	9.95
MARKSON, DAVID. *Wittgenstein's Mistress*	9.95
MOSLEY, NICHOLAS. *Accident*	7.95
MOSLEY, NICHOLAS. *Impossible Object*	7.95
MOSLEY, NICHOLAS. *Judith*	10.95
NAVARRE, YVES. *Our Share of Time*	9.95
QUENEAU, RAYMOND. *The Last Days*	9.95
QUENEAU, RAYMOND. *Pierrot Mon Ami*	7.95
SEESE, JUNE AKERS. *What Waiting Really Means*	7.95
SORRENTINO, GILBERT. *Splendide-Hôtel*	5.95
STEPHENS, MICHAEL. *Season at Coole*	7.95
VALENZUELA, LUISA. *He Who Searches*	8.00
WOOLF, DOUGLAS. *Wall to Wall*	7.95
ZUKOFSKY, LOUIS. *Collected Fiction*	9.95

NONFICTION

MATHEWS, HARRY. *20 Lines a Day*	8.95
ROUDIEZ, LEON S. *French Fiction Revisited*	14.95
SHKLOVSKY, VIKTOR. *Theory of Prose*	12.95

POETRY

ANSEN, ALAN. *Contact Highs: Selected Poems*	11.95
FAIRBANKS, LAUREN. *Muzzle Thyself*	9.95

For a complete catalog of our titles, or to order any of these books, write to Dalkey Archive Press, 5700 College Road, Lisle, IL 60532. One book, 10% off; two books or more, 20% off; add $3.00 postage and handling.